“This l … ined a brilliant story that she instantly brought to life.”— **Spunky N Sassy**, Goodreads.com

“This Romantic Dramedy is wonderfully written. Catrina is both beautiful and flawed, strong in spite of the past horrors. While not as lighthearted as *Caught on Camera*, it still manages to read like your favorite movie you keep in your DVD collection.”— **Yafania T.**, Goodreads.com

“A great read if you like your action, adventure and romance in one funny bundle.”— **Molly**, Goodreads.com

“Neither Cat nor Chett has any interest in a relationship—especially since Cat comes as a package deal with a huge German shepherd and Chett is afraid of dogs. Attraction wins out, but will Cat’s inner traumas (and her big ass dog) and Chett’s drive to get back on top in Hollywood keep them from going beyond a quick affair?...Ms. Morgan keeps the plot moving with humorous situations and dialogue interspersed with exciting and poignant drama. A good read for a snowy afternoon.”— **Marc Joseph**, InD’Tale magazine

HOLLYWOOD IN MUSKOKA 2

Seduced BY THE SCREENWRITER

Madelle Morgan

McBride Publishing Group, Canada

Seduced by the Screenwriter, Hollywood in Muskoka series, Book 2

Published by McBride Publishing Group, 2018
First published to Kindle, 2017

Cover design by Kimberly Killion
Interior design by M. A. Demers

Library and Archives Canada

ISBN 978-1-988917-00-9 (Kindle edition)
ISBN 978-1-988917-01-6 (ePub edition)
ISBN 978-1-988917-02-3 (iBooks edition)
ISBN 978-1-988917-03-0 (paperback)

Order paperback copies in bulk through Ingram or Amazon.

Published in Canada

DEDICATION

This story is dedicated to police officers, firefighters, members of the armed forces, EMTs/paramedics, and other first responders who put their lives on the line on behalf of the rest of us.

ACKNOWLEDGMENTS

I'm very grateful to several people who made this a better book. Lillian Chow was the developmental editor and a beta reader. Her screenwriting training and insightful input after the initial drafts kept me on track. Beta reader Erin Scothorn, an author, indicated where I needed to sharpen Catrina's empowerment journey and the characters' motivations. Retired police officer Marlene M. provided valuable information on Ontario police procedures and police service dogs. My awesome copy editor and formatter M. A. Demers is one of the best in the business.

As a thank-you to all readers, when you subscribe to my occasional newsletter at MadelleMorgan.com for email announcements of new releases, price promotions, and giveaways, you'll receive a free download of my steamy, fun short story *The Next Big Thing*.

Contents

PLAYLIST

Seduced by the Screenwriter has a "soundtrack"! When you see this symbol [♬] in the chapter, listen to the song that accompanies the story. You'll need to listen on your smartphone, laptop, or another device.

Several songs feature these popular artists born in Canada: k.d. lang; Mermaids Exist; The Tenors; Michael Bublé; The Weeknd; Bryan Adams; and Demi Lovato.

Listening to songs while reading the story is optional, but if you'd like to try it, here's how:

Option 1: Create a playlist before starting to read the novel

If you subscribe to a music streaming service or have an account with a music retail store such as iTunes, create a *Seduced by the Screenwriter* playlist on your device using the titles of the songs below. Then when you see [♬] together with the title of a song in the text, listen to that song on your device.

Here are some free options:

Option 2: YouTube videos

Open the playlist page, MadelleMorgan.com/SSplaylist, in your browser to listen to the songs on YouTube.com as you read the novel.

When you see [♬] together with the name of a song in the text, flip to MadelleMorgan.com/SSplaylist and click on the YouTube link for that song.

Option 3: Get Spotify free

Spotify.com has a free option. Create a playlist using the song titles below. However, there is no guarantee that every song will be free on Spotify.

Note: certain songs may not be available in your country on YouTube.com, in the iTunes Store, or from Spotify.com and other music streaming services.

***

"**Baby, It's Cold Outside**," performed by Idina Menzel (duet with Michael Bublé), from her album *Holiday Wishes*.

"**Girls Just Want to Have Fun**," performed by Cyndi Lauper, from the album *She's So Unusual*.

"**Watching Over You**," performed by Holly McNarland, from the film *Men With Brooms*. (YouTube video only.)

"**Dibs**," performed by Kelsea Ballerini, from the album *The First Time*.

"**Sexuality**," performed by k.d. lang, from the album *All You Can Eat*.

"**Little Man**," performed by Mermaids Exist, from the album *Losing Colour*.

"**Kokomo**," performed by The Beach Boys, from the album *Still Cruisin'*.

"**Love Me Harder**," performed by Ariana Grande (duet with The Weeknd), from her album *My Everything*.

"**Speedboat Chase**," video clip from the film *Face/Off* (1997) starring John Travolta and Nicholas Cage. (YouTube video only.)

"**That's Amore**," performed by Dean Martin, from the album *Dean Martin Sings*.

"**Dare to Live**," performed by Andrea Bocelli (duet with Laura Pausini), from his album *The Best of Andrea Bocelli: Vivere*.

"**Lean on Me**," performed by The Tenors, from the album *Under One Sky*.

"**Faith**," performed by Stevie Wonder (featuring Ariana Grande), from the film *Sing*.

"**Cold**," performed by Tears for Fears, from the album *Elemental*.

"**I Finally Found Someone**," performed by Barbra Streisand (duet with Bryan Adams), from the album *The Mirror Has Two Faces*.

"**Goodbye My Lover**," performed by James Blunt, from the album *Back to Bedlam*.

"**Stone Cold**," performed by Demi Lovato, from the album *Confident*.

"**Roar**," performed by Katy Perry, from the album *Prism*.

CHAPTER 1

Baby, It's Cold Outside

A knee-deep layer of fresh snow blocked the long laneway to the five-thousand-square-foot lake house owned by Catrina's most important client, Jenna Jordan, Hollywood movie star.

"It's our lucky day! The plow hasn't been by yet. I'll need the snowshoes, Titan," Catrina informed her German shepherd, who wagged his tail at the thrum of pleasure in her voice. She reached into the cargo area of her beat-up SUV to fish out new aluminum frames.

The awkward foot extensions firmly attached, her down parka zipped, Catrina adopted a wide stance and swung her legs forward, each step a delight as the snowshoe sank a couple of inches into powder. Titan bounded ahead to sniff the tracks of rabbits and deer. Pine and spruce branches sagged with sparkling snow.

The crisp, sunny early January day, the pristine forest, the opportunity to fill her lungs with pure air—they all validated her decision to quit her job as a Toronto Police constable in order to provide security services to millionaire owners of exclusive waterfront properties on Lake Muskoka, Canada's summer playground for the fabulously rich and famous.

No boss. No shifts. No traffic!

Her fledgling stress-free business amounted to a paid vacation year round. So far she had security contracts with ten clients and enough income to pay the bills. Her big break came the previous summer when Jenna signed on as a client after firing the security guard who'd helped himself to several bottles in the wine cellar and let mice roam the interior.

Feeling pleased with the peaceful life she'd created for herself, Catrina hummed a tune that had been playing in the stores nonstop over the recent holiday season:

[♬ "Baby, It's Cold Outside"]

A whiff of wood smoke stopped her short. Jenna's residence was supposed to be vacant. The Hollywood actor never visited between September and June. Now on high alert, Catrina punched rapidly through the snow another quarter mile to a curve that provided a sightline to the main house.

A tendril of smoke indeed curled from the chimney. A faint, rhythmic *thwack, thwack* disrupted the tranquility of the isolated property. She sucked frigid air deep into a tight chest. Titan, sensing the tension in his mistress, growled deep in his throat.

"Quiet," she commanded. "Heel." She silently advanced around the bend, pulled off a thermal-insulated glove to reach inside her goose-down parka, and retrieved the small set of binoculars from an inside pocket. Titan sniffed the air, his nose and ears alerted toward the buildings. His extraordinary sense of smell had picked up something new, something that did not belong.

Thwack. Thwack. The sound of sharp blows echoed across the ice-covered lake beyond the boathouse. Adjusting the focus of the lens, she spied a male figure splitting cordwood behind the three-car garage.

Thwack. Driven by some inner demon, a broad-shouldered man, clad only in jeans and a white T-shirt, was repeatedly raising an axe buried in a log and slamming the end into a stump with a force that shook his lean body. Two pieces of wood catapulted through the air to land several feet away in the snow. The macho demonstration of force triggered memories buried deep. Heart thumping, Catrina fought back nausea, one of the symptoms of her Post-Traumatic Stress Disorder.

Handsome fiend, she decided, peering through the lens at the stranger's sun-streaked brown hair, well-proportioned six-foot-two frame, and a largish nose under thunderous brows. Still, he had to be unhinged to be out in the frigid air without a coat on, splitting logs for no good reason. She'd ensured there was enough dry, split firewood for two winters.

"This guy looks like trouble, Titan. We don't want trouble." She lowered the binoculars, cursing under her breath. She'd moved to Port Carson in Muskoka to avoid having to deal with "incidents."

No way was she approaching this lunatic too close. Not without a weapon. Her left hand slipped into her pocket to clasp the cell phone with 911 on speed dial. Alerted by pheromones in the beaded sweat on his mistress's brow, Titan's muscles bunched as he prepared to lunge at the intruder on her command. Catrina needed to figure out who this guy was before the retired police dog tore a chunk out of the man's tight butt.

Quickly she dialed her contact for the property, Jenna Jordan's personal assistant.

A decidedly grumpy voice answered the summons. "Who the hell is it?"

"Stacey, it's Catrina Turner up in Muskoka. There's someone in the lake house. Did Jenna give anyone the key and alarm code?"

"Do you realize it is—oh my god—six a.m. here in California?" came the angry retort.

Catrina was well aware of the three-hour time difference. She swallowed impatience. "You hired me for security. I'm checking up because there isn't anyone scheduled to be in residence. The alarm didn't activate, but if it's an intruder I'm going to call the police."

"NO! Don't call the cops." Catrina heard noises indicating movement—a series of thuds and muffled curses as Stacey scrambled out of bed. "I, um, meant to send an email. It slipped my mind, what with the Golden Globe Awards next weekend, the party invitations...Jenna's a nominee. Don't tell her I forgot. She'll have my ass. Not that she cares about anything at the moment except fitting into her designer gown."

"So who's the guest?"

"Chett de Groot."

"Who?"

"The screenwriter. Don't piss him off or I'll be fired for sure. Jenna loaned him the lake house with the expectation that he'll write a lead part for her into his next project. If she doesn't win a Golden Globe, Chett's her backup plan. Roles for women in their late thirties are in short supply, and her talent agent is trying to convince Jenna, a sex siren, to accept a role as a *mother*. Can you believe it?"

Without waiting for Catrina's response, the words continued to tumble out. "Her fans won't frigging believe it either. She'll be finished. So listen to me closely. Give Chett de Groot *whatever he wants*. Jenna's career depends on it! *Capisce?*"

"Yes, ma'am. Wait—" The call disconnected.

Catrina tucked the phone back into her pocket. "Well, Titan, we've been given our instructions. I just need to confirm that this guy's the genuine article. That's it for the excitement today."

Which suited her just fine. Situation averted. After handing in her badge and her Glock, she'd obtained a private investigator license but had decided not to apply for a handgun license. She'd built a new life in vacation country specifically to escape criminal violence. On the rare occasion of a break and enter, she called in the Ontario Provincial Police.

If some writer she'd never heard of wanted to hole up alone in a secluded house to write a part for Jenna, Catrina would see if he needed anything and then leave him to it. No doubt he'd go stir crazy and be booked on a flight back to California within a week.

Her enjoyment of the normally uneventful daily security patrol now spoiled, she trudged the rest of the way down the hill to the six-bedroom "cottage" with four bathrooms, a home theatre, and a formal dining room that sat twelve. The "bunkie," a guesthouse with two additional bedrooms, was nestled among the trees a hundred feet farther along the shore.

She plodded stiff-legged toward the man, snowshoes sinking softly into fluffy powder. Thirty feet away she halted. Sensing her apprehension, Titan moved into a protective stance at Catrina's left and barked a sharp warning. At the sound, the man she presumed to be Chett de Groot spun on one cowboy boot, axe at the ready in his right hand.

"This is private property," he shouted, red-faced. "Don't come any closer."

Titan scented fear and barked a warning. Adrenaline coursed through Catrina's veins. She inhaled crisp, bracing air and fought the urge to get the hell out of his space. The stranger was cranky and cold, she told herself sternly, not a deranged axe murderer. For the dog's sake, she needed to radiate calm.

"I'm the security hired to protect this place," she shouted back in her best authoritative cop voice. She extracted a business card from a pocket and waved it at him. “Can I have your name?”

“Chett de Groot.”

Satisfied, she advanced a few steps to get a closer look at his wild eyes and flushed, unshaven mug. “Do you need anything? A parka, perhaps?”

“No. I just want to be left alone. No women. No dogs. Especially no *dogs*.” He gripped the axe handle with two muscular arms and slammed the sharp edge an inch into the stump.

Impressed, and not in a good way, Catrina hastily dropped the card onto the snow.

“Give me a shout if you change your mind. Stacey asked me to help you out.” There, she’d done her duty. With Titan heeling tight to her left, she quickstepped up the long driveway as if her life depended on it.

“Wait. There’s no water.”

Pushing back her fur-trimmed hood, she twisted to confront this new complication. “The place is closed up for the winter. The waterlines were drained in case they froze.”

Catrina sighed, knowing that it’d be a heck of a job to get the home’s well pump going during the coldest month of the winter. She knew for a fact that the plumber had not installed heat trace on the waterlines because the owner had sworn she’d never in a million years set foot in snow unless it was artificial snow on a soundstage.

Perhaps Chett could get by with bottled water and the outhouse. “How long are you staying?”

“Long enough to write a blockbuster screenplay.”

She’d read that a movie screenplay only ran about a hundred pages, most of that dialogue. “A week?”

A reluctant grin slashed the darkness contorting his features. “A month, at least.” The smile disappeared. “Maybe longer,” he admitted.

"You'll need the water, then," she agreed. "The plumber will be on it this afternoon."

"If it's not too much trouble."

The sociable comment threw her. Chett was a real Dr. Jekyll and Mr. Hyde. She cocked her head, considering. This de Groot was either a close friend of Jenna's or an annoyance she wanted as far as possible from L.A. and the voracious paparazzi during the awards season. Still, it was useless to speculate. Shrugging her shoulders, Catrina decided she'd err on the side of caution and be nice to him.

She rotated her snowshoes and trudged a few steps nearer. "Calling a plumber is part of the comprehensive service I provide to my clients. Besides security, I arrange for renovations and maintenance, landscaping, vehicle repair, and even catering."

Keeping a wary eye on the dog, Chett advanced to pick Catrina's business card out of the snow. "Turner and Pooch Security Services?" The barest hint of a smile twitched the corners of his mouth.

"That's us. I'm Catrina Turner." She waved at the dog. "This is Titan. He's a retired police general service dog and great at tracking tourists who get lost in the woods."

Titan gave a happy bark. Chett took a nervous step back. "Does he bite?"

"When provoked."

"Shit." The sweat from the guy's exertions had cooled in the frigid air, and he began to shiver. "I traveled three thousand miles to a place where I can work without any distractions. You and especially that animal don't need to check on the place while I'm living here."

She shook her head. "Oh yes, I do. It's in my contract. Sorry, you're stuck with me for the duration. But Titan and I will stay out of your way."

The hypervigilant part of her psyche was super relieved that he had a dog phobia. If Jenna ever complained that Catrina didn't pay enough attention to Chett de Groot, she had that explanation in her back pocket.

She swiveled clumsily in her snowshoes in another attempt to leave, another attempt to salvage the rest of her day. For the sake of Jenna's career, and thus her ability to pay for Catrina's services, Catrina only needed to keep Chett comfortable for the duration of his visit.

"Buy a parka and gloves," she suggested over her shoulder. "There's no clause in my contract that covers nursing you through pneumonia."

As she crested the slope before the curve in the lane, she chanced a quick glance backward, saw him watching her.

"Next time bring a leash," he yelled.

***

Chett heeded the advice of the attractive dark-haired security guard—in her early thirties, at a guess—and retreated to the warmth of the wood fire blazing in the great room's enormous fieldstone fireplace. Jenna had given him *carte blanche* with respect to the stocked freezer, wine cellar, and bar. The lack of running water was a minor annoyance. He didn't take water in his whisky anyway.

He filled a glass from a half-empty bottle of twelve-year-old golden elixir, sank into the white leather sofa, propped his frozen feet on the distressed pine coffee table, and contemplated his grim situation.

He needed a hit.

The most recent action film with his name attached went straight to DVD. More importantly, it had lost money. Millions. A-list directors and producers had wasted no time deleting his name from their contact lists. Their assistants pretended to lose Chett's messages.

Compounding his predicament as a washed-up screenwriter at thirty-six, his ex-wife had filed for overdue spousal support. He raised his glass to the hot, blond southern princess who'd mutated into the Wicked Witch when the money ran out. *Good luck with that, honey.*

Jenna believed in him. She'd offered him her vacation home up in Canada, convinced the lack of distractions would enable him to focus on writing another hit like *Undercover Slasher*, his bad-cop thriller of five years ago.

Besides, he owed her. He and Jenna went back fifteen years when both had worked in the Beverly Hills Hotel—him behind the bar, her waiting tables. She'd snagged an agent first, got a few walk-ons, and invited him to industry parties as her date. At one party she introduced Chett to a producer who wanted to get into Jenna's pants so bad he agreed to read Chett's screenplay. Eventually the guy dumped Jenna for another ingenue but did option the screenplay.

Jenna had set up Chett's lucky break. He'd sworn on his parents' graves to write a leading role for her.

Of course, he'd neglected to mention his writer's block.

CHAPTER 2

Coffee, Tea, or Me?

At nine the next morning, Chett was waiting for her.

He'd acquired a parka and gloves, Catrina noted approvingly as she parked the SUV beside Jenna's garage. He seemed calmer. Rested. There was no sign of the violent emotions he'd vented while splitting logs twenty-four hours earlier.

Chett opened the driver's door and drew his lips back to expose a blinding set of perfect white teeth in what was intended as a sunny, carefree smile. "Good morning." He eyed the dog in the passenger seat, backed off five feet and continued more loudly. "I need a favor."

Catrina blinked. He'd shaved and showered. Titan's nose twitched as he processed the scent of musky after-shave lotion. The guy cleaned up well, Catrina had to admit. On the other hand, she'd been a cop too long to be swayed by a handsome face.

"Your water's hooked up, the lane is plowed. What more could you want? A ride to the airport?"

Chett's penetrating Caribbean-blue eyes locked on hers, as intent as Titan's when he spied a juicy steak. "Hate to disappoint you, but I'm not leaving. Jenna said I could use one of her vehicles, and you have the keys. Apparently another of your services is to drive her two SUVs occasionally over the winter so they don't seize up. Also, I'm going to drop off my rental car and need a ride back here. How about it?"

"Sure, no problem." She slid out of her vehicle. "Okay, I'll meet you in Port Carson at the car rental depot. Before

I leave here I'll do a security sweep and set the alarm."

"You don't trust me."

He had that right. "Jenna pays me, not you," she crisply reminded him.

After Chett reversed his rental car out of the garage's third bay and drove up the hill and out of sight, Catrina texted Stacey for verification that Chett was authorized to use Jenna's vehicles.

***

Twenty minutes later, after dropping Titan off at home, Catrina pulled into the rental car lot. To her surprise, Chett wasn't waiting for her inside the heated office. Instead, he appeared to be having a conversation with an attendant who'd ducked outside for a smoke.

Catrina tapped the horn. When Chett pulled open the front passenger door, he peered warily into the back seat and rear compartment. No dog. This time a genuine smile punched cute dimples into his tanned cheeks. Her heart jerked. Jeez, she had such a girly weakness for dimples.

He slid in and buckled his seat belt. Shifting into forward, she swung the vehicle around and turned onto the road leading to the village Main Street shops.

"You didn't even pull up your hood back there. Are you trying to catch your death?"

Chett aimed a cheerful grin her way. "So you *do* care."

"You need to write that screenplay, remember?" And the sooner he finished it, the sooner she could return to her peaceful routine.

At the reminder, Chett's smile dissolved into a grimace. "How cold is it, anyway? The weather report on the car radio said minus fifteen Celsius. What's that in Fahrenheit?"

"Five degrees. It's typical for January in Canada, but your constitution isn't acclimatized to this cold."

"It's invigorating."

Catrina slanted a baleful glance in his direction and sniffed the air a couple of times. "Have you been drinking? It's not yet ten o'clock, for God's sake."

"What are you, a cop?" he asked, glaring at her.

"An ex-cop, as a matter of fact," she shot back.

"*That* explains it."

"Explains what?"

"Your attitude." He nodded. "Cop attitude."

"Excuse me?" She slammed on the brakes at a stop sign and sucked in a calming breath. She refused to let this arrogant visitor push her buttons, dimples or no dimples. "You need to get back to work," she barked. "First I'm going to pour some coffee into you, sober you up."

He threw up his hands. "I have not been drinking…this morning. I was simply asking that car jockey what men do for excitement around here."

"You want to know what men do around here? Canadians go to Timmy's for their coffee breaks, and it's that time of day." She pulled into the Tim Hortons parking lot.

Inside, the lineup stretched from the counter all the way to the entrance. The District of Muskoka's year-round residents enjoyed a laid-back lifestyle, especially in winter, and they appreciated the time to chat and catch up on local gossip with their neighbors.

Finally a muscular, tattooed dude in his early twenties with "Bob Ryerson, Assistant Manager" on his name tag asked for their order.

"Bob, I'll have my usual, an extra-large Double-double." Catrina swiveled to Chett behind her. "The same?"

"What's a Double-double? It's not on the menu."

"He's American," she announced to Bob—and by extension to all the eavesdroppers in line behind them.

Although big Hollywood names, along with their families, friends and hangers-on, flocked to their upscale waterfront homes every summer, the area didn't get too many tanned tourists in midwinter. To Chett she explained, "A Double-double is a coffee with two creams and two sugars."

"You an actor?" Bob asked over one bulging bicep as he poured Catrina's coffee into a paper cup.

"Chett de Groot, screenwriter," came the answer. "And I believe I'll try a Double-double. When in Rome—"

"No shit!" Bob's pleasant round face broke into a wide grin. "Whoa, man, I know who you are! You wrote *Undercover Slasher* and *Mafia Massacre*. An extra-large coffee is on me if you'll sign this serviette, and I'll throw in a couple of Timbits. My treat." Bob shoved a napkin across the counter, slapped a pen on top, then turned to select bite-size glazed balls from the wall rack filled with baskets of donuts, cookies, and pastries.

To avoid being plagued by questions for the rest of the week, Catrina proceeded to satisfy the curiosity of the locals whispering in line behind them, well aware that the Timmy's crowd would spread the word on social media. "Mr. de Groot is staying at Jenna Jordan's place for the peace and quiet to work on a new screenplay. He needs to be left alone to concentrate."

The napkin was duly signed and pinned to a wall plastered with autographed scraps of paper and photos of various comedians, actors, famous athletes, and other greats of the entertainment and sports worlds who'd visited Muskoka. Catrina found them a table near the window.

Chett shrugged out of his parka and hung it on the back of his chair. "Who is Tim Horton, anyway?"

Catrina stacked cold hands around her twenty-four-ounce coffee cup—the best hand warmer ever. "Tim

Horton was a National Hockey League defenseman who established a coffee and baked goods franchise that spread across Canada and into the U.S. The Canadian forces camp in Afghanistan even had an outlet." She watched him check out the other customers giving him the once-over. "Timmy's serves breakfast and lunch, too. It's a popular meeting spot."

Chett popped a Timbit into his mouth. His brows lifted. "It's a donut."

"Supposedly Timbits are donut holes, made from the dough punched out of the center of donuts," she corrected.

Chett glanced around. "So men hang out here. What else do Canadian men do all winter?"

Catrina shrugged. "Well, hockey is Canada's national sport. Guys around here live and breathe the game. At our local brew pub owned by a former NHL superstar right winger, you'd better not be a Montreal Canadians or Ottawa Senators fan, or for that matter a fan of any hockey team other than the Toronto Maple Leafs." She sipped her Double-double. "Evenings when there's no hockey game on TV, men watch home renovation shows, and then on Saturdays go to Canadian Tire, our national hardware and sporting goods chain, to buy tools for projects they'll never finish."

Chett chuckled. Encouraged, she continued. "Men coach kids' hockey or yell at the referees from the arena stands. For recreation they ice fish, go snowmobiling, or curl."

"If their men are out fishing and such with their bros," Chett asked, "what kind of attention do the local women get?" The aforesaid local women in the coffee shop eyed him curiously, but he ignored them, his blue eyes fixed exclusively on Catrina.

She frowned. "Not much. The only action women see during hockey season involves ten skaters fighting for a puck. I bet the birth stats prove that hardly any Canadian babies are conceived during the Stanley Cup Playoffs."

"I don't know how to play any of those winter sports." He leaned forward and said in a low tone that wouldn't be overheard, "And I prefer my recreational activities to include women, preferably indoors in this abominable cold." He considered. "Although sex in the snow would be a first. I could be persuaded."

She choked, coughed. Hot coffee dribbled down her chin. Was that a proposition? "By me?" she sputtered, patting a serviette over her face and shirtfront. "Not interested," she added, refusing to look at him because her response was a blatant lie.

Stacey had ordered Catrina to fill de Groot's every need, but she drew the line at warming the bed of a tightly wound Hollywood hunk with an axe. Then as they chatted over coffee, her resolve to avoid the intriguing visitor had begun to melt like an icicle under a warm sun.

Most of the local men had partners, and any unattached males were single for a reason. She'd been celibate for over a year since moving to Port Carson, and until this minute had not realized how much she missed male companionship. She was starving, and across from her a guy with adorable dimples was offering a no-strings, love 'em and leave 'em buffet. On the downside, if she distracted him too much he'd never finish Jenna's screenplay.

He tapped the table to get her attention. "Are you seeing someone?"

She shrugged. "No. You'd find that out soon enough anyway. But that's not the reason why we shouldn't…get involved."

He propped his elbows on the table and leaned in with an invitation to confide. "Tell me why a beautiful woman like you is single."

A committed relationship was not possible with this visitor or anyone else for that matter, but Catrina had no intention of revealing why. "You need to focus on writing," she said firmly. "Jenna is counting on you, and her success keeps me employed."

Perceptive blue eyes bore into hers. "What's your life like in Port Carson, then? All work and no play?"

Apparently her neglected libido had handed over a permission slip, because he persisted. "How about if I combine work and play? I'll write some love scenes, and you act them out with me. It'll help me to get the creative juices flowing."

She sighed, weakening. "You aren't writing another cop movie, are you? Because I'm so done with that. I left the force to get away from all reminders of—" She halted, shook her head. She never spoke of the underwater deaths that haunted her. Not to anyone. "Being a cop, a real cop, not those fake cops in your movies, is not entertaining."

He turned his hands palm up. "It's what I write. Action flicks put twelve- to twenty-four-year-old males into movie theater seats."

A crushing sensation squeezed her lungs. "You haven't *lived* it. Dealing with violence, horrific accidents, and...and dead bodies every day takes its toll. Physically. Emotionally. Mentally." She sucked in a breath, then let it out slowly to relieve the gut-tightening anxiety that made her nauseous when memories of the traumatic recovery dive surfaced. She needed to keep them buried, because the alternative meant loss of emotional control. She straightened her spine and gave him a logical reason. "Those car chase and shoot 'em up movies don't attract women—half the potential audience—unless they have heart."

"I have no heart." His tone dripped acid. "My ex took

it along with my Porsche and stock portfolio when she dumped me."

A rare chuckle slipped past Catrina's guard. "See, you *can* be funny. Write a romantic comedy that makes me laugh, and I'll do it."

The solitary days and long Muskoka winter nights with no male but Titan to keep Catrina company were getting to her. She needed to lighten up and have some fun. Besides, by agreeing to playact she could keep an eye on Chett, make sure he was writing and not drinking his way through the bottles stacked in Jenna's bar and wine cellar.

Chett demurred. "If you were serious about helping me craft a new screenplay, you'd go with the cop scenario. Being an ex-cop and all, you could be my technical adviser." He leaned in to emphasize his next words. "I don't know a damn thing about writing comedy. Action scripts are what I do."

She leaned across the table and, nose to nose, stared straight into his baby blues. "How's that working for you lately?"

He winced, withdrew. "Ouch. Right, you win. I'll give it a shot."

She rolled her eyes at his word choice and folded her arms. "No guns. No fighting. Or I walk."

He capitulated and reached across to shake her hand. "Deal."

As she'd anticipated, the prospect of sex won out. He was a red-blooded man who'd experienced the boredom of a long, dark, freezing night in the boonies.

"Are you free tomorrow night, say at eight?" he continued. "That will give me enough time to write a scene or two."

She nodded. "Titan and I are available."

His skin paled under the tan. "You're bringing the beast? You realize that may affect the, ah, performance?"

She snickered, relaxed, and shoved the chair back. "That reminds me, I have some rules."

"Of course a cop has rules."

"I'm not a cop anymore, remember? These are dating rules." She glanced from side to side to check for eavesdroppers, raised her butt from the chair to lean across the table, and whispered for his ears only, "No sex on the first date. No overnights." In a normal voice she added, "And yes, Titan and I are a two-for-one deal."

Disappointment filled in Chett's dimples. Catrina didn't know whether it was due to her rules or his fear of dogs. Not that she wanted to put a damper on the fun, but Chett's bottled-up frustration made her wary. Titan helped her feel safe.

Fun. She hungered for some of the intimate persuasion. Then in a month or so Chett would return to California. No complications. This could be a win-win proposition for both of them.

Standing, she drained the last of her coffee and used her thumbs to unroll the rim of the paper cup to reveal the word *WINNER*. She'd won a free cup of coffee!

She took it as a sign that her luck was changing.

[♫ "Girls Just Want To Have Fun"]

CHAPTER 3

Lust in Space

Chett watched Catrina read the first page of the scene, then the second. Watched a frown knit her brows together in a glower—not the reaction he wanted from a woman he planned to seduce.

"This is sci-fi," she accused. "It's not romantic comedy."

"It's intended to be comedy. Sci-fi comedy." When she turned her cynical cop eye on him, he said defensively, "This scene was inspired by *Lost in Space*. You must admit that movie is hilarious." He pointed at the green unitard with iridescent scales that was flung over the back of the sofa. "I found this lizard outfit and other costumes in a guest room walk-in closet."

As she inspected the one piece, an embarrassed flush stained her high cheekbones. "There's no crotch," she exclaimed.

"It's not what you think. Jenna needed a way to pee between takes."

Catrina didn't seem convinced. "I may need some lubrication."

"There's no intercourse in the scene as promised."

"I meant of the alcohol variety," she said dryly.

He moved to the wine fridge. "Your wish is my command."

She waved the script. "According to this, it's the other way around."

He laughed and handed her a glass. "Award-winning Chardonnay," he said as she sniffed the bouquet, tasted the wine and nodded with appreciation. "Straight from Napa Valley by way of Jenna's wine cellar."

He leaned one elbow on the kitchen island's granite counter, amused by her reaction to the expensive wine. He felt relaxed for the first time in weeks. Writing the campy scene had relieved numbing pressure to draft the genuine article. Even the sight of the massive canine sprawled in front of the crackling fire failed to dampen his mood.

While sipping the wine, Catrina scanned the remaining five pages of the script. "I'm ready," she announced in due course as she set her empty glass on the island.

"You'll need to put on your costume," he noted.

She waved at his black jeans and T-shirt. "Where's yours?"

"I'm Dan East, space pilot. This is my uniform for exploring planets in Xenon Galaxy. Besides, Jenna only kept her personal costumes. There are no outfits for men."

"I should have added 'no slave girls' to the list of rules," she grumbled as she grabbed the costume and climbed the staircase to the bedroom level.

"You're not a slave girl, you're a female lizard-like alien," he called after her.

"With no lines to learn."

"The lizards can't speak English," he retorted as a second-floor door slammed. "And in this sci-fi scenario the universal translator hasn't been invented yet," he explained to Titan.

Five minutes later Catrina emerged onto the landing and slinked down the stairs.

Wow! Chett's jaw slackened. His surroundings faded. Hell, he even forgot about the dog. Nothing existed but Lizard Girl, all boobs and sweetly curved ass and long, lean legs in the skintight suit, hair tucked under a form-fitting hood. Except Catrina's luscious breasts straining the stretchy fabric were natural, unlike Jenna's. That damn parka had hidden a body that had his member powered up and ready for lift off.

"Looks great," he choked, sinking into the sofa to hide his erection. Then he shifted, realizing that he'd inadvertently sat on the dog's dialogue. From under his butt he pulled several cardboard rectangles with loops of string stapled to the corners. "Titan is the robot character. Can you hang these around his neck?"

With a puzzled woof, Titan got to his feet to accept the strange collar from Catrina, then slumped onto the hearth rug with a thud that shook the hardwood floor.

Chett pulled his copy of the script out of his back pocket and described the scene setup to his cast. Lizard Girl had been injured in a vicious skirmish with a cluster of rival lizards and had subsequently been cruelly abandoned by her own kind. Dan East had rescued her and nursed her back to health in a cave while the robot kept watch at the entrance. As the scene opens, Dan is preparing to return to his spaceship to escape this dangerous planet. The enemy lizards, however, have tracked their location. Dan and Lizard Girl are trapped.

Catrina bent her head to memorize the dialogue and action.

```
                    ROBOT
          Warning! Warning!

                  DAN EAST
          Lizard Girl, our only
          chance is to stay hidden
          until the bloodthirsty
          reptiles give up and leave.

    Lizard Girl advances toward Dan East on
    her hind legs, her front claws raised
    and jaws wide.

                  DAN EAST
          Wha-what are you doing?
```

ROBOT
Danger, Dan East!

Lizard Girl pins Dan in her arms and licks his face.

DAN EAST
(face a mask of horror, he struggles to escape)
No! Your lizard poison will paralyze me from the neck down. I'll be at your mercy. After all I've done for you, please don't eat me.

Dan slumps to the floor of the cave as the poison takes effect.

Lizard Girl changes her mind about eating Dan and instead kisses him.

"Okay, let's rehearse. Take 1. Cue the robot," Chett directed.

"Here, Titan," Catrina ordered. Titan obediently lurched to his feet, wandered over and allowed her to remove the top blank card. Thick black letters on the exposed card spelled "Warning! Warning!" She snickered and removed it in readiness for the robot's next line.

Chett recited his line from memory. "Lizard Girl, our only chance is to stay hidden until the vicious reptiles give up and leave."

"Bloodthirsty." Catrina tapped her script. "*Bloodthirsty* reptiles. Distracted or something?"

"Or something," Chett muttered, his erection straining against his zipper. *Man, she's hot.*

Lizard Girl advanced toward Dan, teeth bared.

He gasped, stepped back, and it was no act. Her fierce expression uncomfortably called to mind Titan's massive choppers. Rewrite needed.

"Wha-what are you doing?" Out of the side of his mouth he whispered, "Cue the robot."

She removed the card strung around Titan's neck. "Danger, Dan East!" read the dialogue on the card underneath. Giggling, Lizard Girl removed the card and pointed to the fireplace. "Go lie down," she told the beast.

Titan lumbered to the hearth, head down. *Strange humans. No treat.*

Lizard Girl grabbed Dan's upper arms, stuck out her tongue and licked his chin.

"No!" he exclaimed. "Your lizard poison will paralyze me from the neck down. I'll be at your mercy. After all I've done for you, please don't eat me."

With exaggerated twists and groans, and one eye on the "robot," Chett folded his legs to lay flat on his back on the thick area rug, getting comfortable for the "lizard kiss."

Lizard Girl bent over him, her generous breasts temptingly within reach. Chett cursed himself for writing action that prevented him from moving. He'd wanted her to have fun with being the aggressor, wanted to let her lead. He had never expected the no-nonsense ex-cop to be so *irresistible.*

Lizard Girl's tongue flicked over her lips, watched his gaze clamp to her bust like a magnet to metal. Smirking, she cupped her hands under each breast and adjusted them. Chett moaned. She ran a forefinger down his nose to his mouth, traced its outline, and pulled down his bottom lip. With a hiss, she lowered her body over his, the tips of her breasts grazing his chest, and extended her tongue. She tasted his lips, slid along his teeth, dipped in and out of his mouth.

At the brink of losing self-control, Chett gamely resisted the urge to pull her down and crush her mouth to his. It was her scene.

With a sudden move, she pushed his T-shirt up to his neck, ducked down and licked his nipples.

"That's not in the script," he whispered, reluctant to break character. He'd prescribed kissing, nothing more, for his own selfish reasons. In the back of his mind he'd been worried that Titan might eviscerate him if he made any moves that triggered the dog's protective instincts. The threat chilled Chett's desire to exploit how Catrina was taking this scene a little further than he'd anticipated.

She raised her head and drew a breath. "I'm improvising," she whispered back. "Got any complaints?"

She dipped her lizard head to swipe a long, wet, agile tongue down his bare chest toward his belt buckle, dropping small sucking kisses at intervals. Floods of nerve-buzzing sparks descended in waves to the bulging rocket straining at the jeans encasing his crotch.

"Nah," he moaned. "I'm open to this rewrite."

She slid down to lay along the length of him, her free hand running splayed, probing fingers over his chest, his biceps, his abs while she distracted him with searing, deep kisses. Tongue tangled tongue as each explored the other's warm and wet space.

Heaven help him, Lizard Girl had him as hard as an asteroid. No human male could resist this onslaught. He abandoned any attempt to remember his lines. Lizard Girl had taken the flimsy scene in a much more intriguing direction. This tantalizing woman had passion and a voluptuous body hot enough to melt the ice in the rings around Saturn. He felt privileged—no, obligated—to pilot her to the outer limits of pleasure.

He made a sudden move to reverse their positions on the rug.

A blast of doggy breath washed over his face. Chett turned his head to find himself nose to Titan's quivering nostrils. Instantly Chett's heated blood supercooled.

Red alert! Abort mission! Abort!

In a comet-like flash, Chett rolled Catrina off to the side and shot to his feet, miraculously recovered from the "paralysis."

"Lizard Girl," he yelped, "I'm transporting you to higher ground." Heart pumping at the speed of light, he inserted two hands under her arms, heaved her up with adrenaline-fueled strength and swung her over to the sofa. Weak-kneed, he collapsed onto the soft leather beside her.

Titan cocked his massive head. The card around his neck read, "This does not compute."

Catrina snorted with amusement. Chett breathed deeply, letting the air out in a *whoosh*. Crisis averted. *Damn* this childhood fear of dogs. *Titan was simply curious,* he told himself. Still, his body powered down from "All Systems Go" to "Standby."

"Go lay down," Catrina commanded. Satisfied his mistress was safe, the German shepherd ambled back to the hearth.

Catrina sensuously draped her torso across Chett's lap, barring his escape to a Titan-free zone. One long arm slid up his back under his shirt, fingers cool on his heated skin, while the other arm snaked around his neck to pull his mouth down to hers. Their heartbeats thumped discordantly against each other's chests. She kissed him deep and long until the tension held in his body due to his scare flowed into semi-arousal. Until their heartbeats synced.

Her soft, inviting mouth had many facets, he decided. Her agile lips and tongue could comfort, distract, stimulate, probe, and tease. It was as if she read him, even manipulated his response through the touch of her sensitive lips to his. Lost in delicious sensation, he briefly wondered if he had a similar impact on her. Lizard Girl had slithered into his psyche and charmed her master.

An hour later they broke apart, sighed, stretched.

"I've never necked this long without going all the way," Catrina purred. "My skin's all tingly and extraordinarily sensitive. I feel wonderful."

"Me too." It was true, he realized. His skin seemed to shimmer with heightened response to the most casual caress—a new sensory experience that he put down to never having devoted more than fifteen minutes to foreplay. "Thank you, Lizard Girl, for your assistance in discovering this phenomenon."

She pushed herself to a sitting position. "That sounds like a cue to cut. We didn't stick to the script. Next time—"

He shook his head. "Next time I'll write a different scenario."

"One more suited to your work," she suggested with that irritating tendency she had for reminding him of his obligations.

Lightly, as if it didn't matter, as if his entire future didn't depend on it, he admitted, "I have no idea what to write for Jenna. She's not known as a mature kickass babe like Halle Berry in *X-Men* or Ming-Na Wen in *Agents of S.H.I.E.L.D.*"

Catrina peeled back her lizard costume hood. Thick, dark waves tumbled loose to her shoulders. "You, me, Jenna—we're all reinventing ourselves at this stage of our lives." She punched him lightly in the upper arm. "Don't look so glum all of a sudden. Any scene that gets the words flowing and blood pumping is fine by me. But make it fun, like tonight."

She bounced off the sofa and asked him to pull down the tiny tab at her neck that betrayed the hidden zipper.

As he complied he observed, "In costume, people actually reveal more about themselves than they realize. They feel freer to express who they really are."

Catrina's shoulders drew in tightly, like his did when he was too close to Titan for comfort. Facing away from him, she kept her tone casual. Too casual. "What did I reveal?"

He bent to her neck and inhaled the enticing floral scent she'd spritzed behind her ears. "That beneath your no-nonsense exterior, you're playful, sensual, intuitive, and highly tuned to people. You read me like a book."

Her shoulders relaxed. Clearly delighted, she swiveled to kiss him on the nose. "What a charismatic man you can be when not swinging an axe. I do believe even Titan likes you."

Chett forced himself to look over at the enormous animal stretched the width of the fireplace, pointed ears alert at the sound of his name, and shuddered. Tonight had made it clear that, unless he could get over his physical reaction to Titan, he had zero chance of completing the mission.

Shit.

Fear trumped lust. She and the beast that scared him limp were a team. She'd never give Titan up for a short affair with a stranger. Better to back off now, before he disappointed her and humiliated himself.

He'd reluctantly decided on a polite, noncommittal "I'll call you" brush-off when Catrina made a suggestion no red-blooded man could refuse.

"Will you write another scene for us? I want a romantic scene this time, but not men's idea of romantic. I don't want to be a harem girl or Princess Leia on a leash. Women enjoy escapism too." She smoothed her hands sensuously down the sides of her breasts and over the curves of her hips. His pulse ratcheted up a couple of degrees on the dial.

"A costume that's removable would be nice," she hinted in a deliberately husky drawl that tightened his groin.

Chett was all for getting naked with Catrina. A night of passionate lovemaking was feasible, he reasoned, as long as her dog stayed far, far away.

"It's a deal, on one condition." He twisted a strand of her soft shoulder-length hair around one finger and gazed directly into her intelligent brown eyes. "There won't be a role for Titan. He's got to be off the 'set,' behind a closed door, or preferably at home."

She tipped her head to acknowledge she understood the request and the reason for it. "No problem."

"Is tomorrow night good for you?"

Disappointment pushed out her delectable, slightly swollen bottom lip. "Sorry, I have a curling game. I play in a mixed league." Her face brightened. "Hey, you could fill in for our lead! He's out with the flu."

"I'm not sure about lead. Seems important. What if I took the rear position?"

She laughed. "Lead is the best position for newbies. The more experienced players can knock out any poorly placed rocks."

He considered. On the one hand he'd have the opportunity to get to know the intriguing Catrina better without the Hound of the Baskervilles at her side. On the other hand, he had no clue how to play the game. "What would I have to do?"

"Curling is imported from Scotland and involves sliding forty-pound granite rocks down a sheet of ice to a bull's-eye target called 'the house.' The strategy is to knock the other team's rocks out of the house so that your team's rocks are closest to the center of the house, called 'the button.'"

"Shuffleboard on ice." He nodded. "I can manage that."

After she'd changed and donned her parka, Catrina paused in the frigid air at the open door. She threw her arms around Chett in a bear hug.

"However our stories unfold," she whispered, "I'll know your kisses for life." As she passed through the door into the deep black of a starless night, she saucily promised over one shoulder, "Meet me at the curling club at seven tomorrow night, and I'll help you get your rocks off."

He grinned. "Now *that's* an exit line!"

CHAPTER 4

Getting His Rocks Off

To prepare for his second date with Catrina in a few hours, Chett watched the quintessential Canadian curling movie, *Men with Brooms*, and searched the Internet for a description of the game.

An hour and two scotch whiskies later, he had the curling lingo and rules down pat. He realized that, to avoid embarrassing himself in front of strangers, he'd need to practice turning the handle in the direction he wanted the smooth, round granite stone to curve or "curl" down the ice. Simultaneously he had to shove the polished rock just hard enough for it to come to a stop within the bull's-eye painted under the ice at the other end of the game surface.

Chett had no intention of becoming a laughing stock in Muskoka. Bad enough that dozens of film critics had done him that favor back in L.A. Therefore, he arrived to practice half an hour before the scheduled seven p.m. game, only to be disappointed that the four lanes, or "sheets," of ice were occupied with games in progress.

Chett settled in a chair behind the long window separating the curling club lounge from the ice lanes. He observed the technique of a middle-aged man in a bulky knitted cardigan as he crouched to throw a curling rock. The skip stood at the opposite end of the sheet, positioned behind three granite rocks clustered inside the target. He held a long-handled curling brush vertical for aim, and flung an arm out to one side to indicate the direction of the rock's curl.

"How's the line from your end?" the skip called.

"Line's good." The curler raised and poised his body like a sprinter at the starting line, his right hand on the handle of the rock, a brush under his left arm for balance. He pushed off with his right foot from the "hack," a plastic footrest embedded into the ice. Man and rock slid in unison for a few feet until he released the rock with a slight twist to the handle. Two teammates slid alongside the rock as it rumbled along the pebbled sheet.

The skip shouted, "Yes! Hurry. Hurry hard!"

All hell broke loose. The two sweepers leaned on their brushes and furiously polished a path along the ice, careful not to touch the rock. According to the movie, Chett recalled, touching, or "burning," a rock in motion disqualified it.

"Stop!" the skip commanded.

The sweepers fell away. The curler's rock slammed into the three sitting rocks with a *crack, crack, crack* like gunshots. Momentum scattered the rocks outside the outer ring and out of play, leaving the "house" empty.

"Nice triple takeout!" shouted the skip as he used a foot to nudge four rocks into their respective corners.

Apparently a triple takeout was a very good thing, because it was followed by a great deal of backslapping and congratulations.

"Despite first impressions, curling is a rather complex strategic game," said a familiar husky voice close to Chett's ear.

Catrina's sudden appearance jolted his cynical heart. Blood pulsed in his ears.

Her grin acknowledged his startled reaction. "They called me Cat at police college."

Cat. It suited her. Dark, lean-limbed, sinuous. Pretty. Graceful movements. Today she wore black leggings topped with a thigh-length cream wool sweater and thin leather gloves, her shiny dark hair in a ponytail.

The two all-male teams reconnoitered at the lounge end of the ice sheet and shook hands. Chett scowled and stiffened, wondering whether any of those men had intimate knowledge of the smoking figure hidden beneath Catrina's oversized sweater.

"Now they'll all head for the Brew Pub," Catrina observed. "The custom is for the winning team to buy the losing team's drinks."

Chett tried to relax his hiked shoulders. Catrina's love life wasn't any of his business. "So the losers aren't really losers because they score free drinks?"

"Everybody's happy," she agreed. She turned her incisive gaze on him, but misread the reason for the tension in his body. "No one will care if you're the worst curler *ever*. It's a recreational league. Our mixed team has no hope of qualifying for the Brier," she said, referring to Canada's televised national competitive curling competition.

A kernel of an idea for conflict between a flawed movie hero and his female partner/love interest distracted Chett from the jealous tentacles squeezing his balls as he watched the male curlers slide over the ice to the exit. Men's testosterone-driven behavior overpowered logic when it came to women. A female detective might analyze a situation from a different angle than her male colleague, hence generating conflict. And Jenna would make a statuesque female cop.

Chett finally had a spark of a movie concept to develop. Relief slackened the tension in his jaw. He'd feared that his well of creativity had dried up for good. He set aside the idea in order to focus on the game. He certainly did not want to gain a reputation among the locals of being the worst curler ever.

***

Catrina watched Chett glower at the curlers leaving the ice, chewed her bottom lip and wondered where his thoughts had taken him. If he were so afraid of looking incompetent in front of the other men, maybe it hadn't been such a great idea to convince him to sub for their lead.

Men had such fragile egos. Catrina had no intention of inflating his by mentioning how hot he looked in an aged leather bomber jacket and tight jeans. It wasn't typical curling attire, but it would sure please blond, curvy Brigit Becker, Catrina's friend and teammate who owned the SereniTea Shoppe and catering business. Fortunately Brigit was currently dating tall, broad-shouldered Brad Scott, owner of the Port Carson Boat Works and the team's skip. Catrina had Chett all to herself and intended to keep it that way.

Anticipation. The ribald fantasies plaguing her since she reluctantly left for home and Titan the previous night had her innards squirming beneath a cop-calm facade. His big hands on her bare skin. Those agile lips tugging her nipples. His rock-hard member in her wet—she wanted him. Bad.

She pulled her heavy sweater away from hot skin and tingling breasts and looked around the lounge at the players gathering for the next games.

OMG, if I don't get hold of myself, I'll come right in front of these people. She needed to cool off fast, and the curling rink was the place to do it.

Catrina tugged on Chett's elbow. "Let's throw some rocks." She peered at his feet. "You wore runners. Smart move. The leather soles of those cowboy boots of yours are too slippery for curling."

Down on the recently vacated sheet, she coached Chett on releasing the rocks until he got a feel for the weight and power needed to reach the house. Brad, Brigit, and the four members of the opposing team joined them and the game started.

During the game Chett demonstrated a natural athleticism, catching on quickly by imitating the others' techniques. Still, they lost by six points. The lead must do a lot of sweeping, and Chett's domestic skills left a lot to be desired. He burned two rocks. But so what? The man had a sense of humor, killer abs, and was writing a love scene just for her.

[♫ "Watching Over You"]

At the end of the ten-end game, Chett looked at the scoreboard and sighed, the defeat adding to the pile pressing on his soul—a failed marriage and a half dozen rejected scripts. He *hated* losing. Guilt crawled around his gut. He'd buy a round to make up for letting his team down. Maybe two.

Brad clapped Chett on the back. "Don't look so defeated, man. It's only a game."

"Yeah, well in L.A. playing the game is everything. There are winners and there are losers, and you're lower than dirt if you lose."

"Muskoka is a refuge from La La Land," Brad commented flatly. "Isn't that why you're here? The same rules don't apply. From my point of view you're a winner." He nodded at Catrina crouched in the hack, one hand holding the rock handle, a foot sliding along the ice as she prepared to push the stone down toward the starting end in readiness for the curlers' next game. "Cat's sure got it bad. Couldn't take her eyes off you the entire game. I need some of that for me and Brigit. What's your secret?"

Chett knew precisely what had turned *him* on the previous evening. "Costumes," he revealed. "Jenna Jordan's got a closet full of 'em."

Brad nodded wisely. "Women and clothes. Gotcha."

"I've got competition, though." Chett attempted to sound humorously casual.

"No way," Brad insisted. "Cat's been solo since she moved here."

"It's Titan," Chett groused.

Brad chuckled. "Old Titan's her security blanket. We suspect Catrina got spooked when she worked in the city. She won't talk about it, but it must've been bad."

Chett dropped all pretense of making light of his fear of the German shepherd. "That animal is trained to kill!"

"Only on command." With an amused snort, Brad swung his arm across Chett's shoulders and propelled him past Catrina and down the edge of the sheet toward the warmth of the lounge. "Keep his mistress happy and you'll have nothing to worry about, my friend."

Not worry? The woman owned a creature as terrifying as Stephen King's Cujo. Chett was tempted to retort that he was living proof of the lengths a brave man would go to sleep with a beautiful woman, but swallowed the words in a throat tight with intractable fear. No way did he ever want to experience the lengths a trained attack dog would go to protect his mistress.

Chett shuffled in his sneakers through several inches of powdery snow as he, his teammates, and the four curlers on the opposing team crossed Main Street to the Muskoka Laker Brew Pub. Inside a large room with a beamed ceiling, the group snagged a raw-edge wood table beside the gas fireplace. The polished copper-clad bar with nostalgic pulls for draft beer was the public face of a working brewery. An interior window behind the bar gave patrons a view of the origin of the beer in their glasses—large copper vertical tanks connected by shiny pipes.

After all had filled their glasses from the pitcher of

beer bought by the winning team, introductions were shouted over the play-by-play from the hockey game on the plasma screens suspended in two corners of the room. Upon discovering the novice curler was in fact the screenwriter for *Mafia Massacre*, Chett's excited male tablemates insisted on hearing how he developed scripts for his movies, while the women ogled him.

Under normal circumstances Chett considered himself an ace at self-promotion, with many anecdotes at his fingertips about Hollywood actors and his inspiration for the thrilling scenes he'd written. After one story about a fiery car crash sequence gone wrong during filming, he sensed the discomfort in Catrina's body hunched over her beer in the wood chair to his left.

Chett drained his glass and set it down. "Sorry folks. The keyboard is calling me. I have an important scene to write, and I do my best work at night." He winked at Catrina, drawing forth a smile as weak as American beer. He pulled out his wallet and tossed a couple of twenties onto the table. "Next round's on me."

"Titan needs to be let out." Catrina said her goodbyes, pushed back from the table and followed Chett outside.

While they'd been in the bar, thick flakes had carpeted every surface with several more inches of fluffy snow. In anticipation of the snowfall, patrons had propped their vehicle wipers straight out from the windshields. Chett did a double take at the rows of snow-covered cars with black "antennae," huddled in silent formation like an army of giant white insects.

After they crossed the empty street to the curling rink parking lot, Catrina paused to fill her lungs with frigid air. Turned to him. Politely asked if he'd enjoyed the evening. Curling-stone-cold eyes seemed to dwell on thoughts that pulled her into a grim abyss to which he had no access.

Brad had let slip that something in Catrina's past spooked her. He cursed himself for telling the story of the car pileup scene, for inadvertently triggering dark memories. As a cop, she must have attended many horrific real life accidents.

He wanted to give her a hug, but said only, "I really do intend to write tonight. A dry spell has had me worried, I admit, but writing that *Lust in Space* scene broke the dam, so to speak. You're my inspiration."

Then she did look at him, white flakes melting on dark lashes, distracted from old fears as he'd intended.

"*Dry* spell?" She quirked a brow.

"Dry spell with whisky chaser. Satisfied?"

One corner of her mouth lifted. He leaned in to kiss the echo of a smile. She tipped up her chin and pressed cold lips to his. "I had fun again tonight," she murmured. "You're good for me. Sensitive."

"Alpha male," he corrected sternly, and, wrapping one arm around her bulky parka for support, he bent her backward and kissed her thoroughly to prove it.

Her tense lips warmed under his touch, softened. Her mouth opened to allow his tongue to slide in, taste and tangle. Her hood fell away. He opened his eyes to watch white snowflakes land on her dark hair, melt on curved, cold-reddened skin, and glitter in snow-softened golden light from the streetlamps. He knew he'd cherish this hauntingly beautiful memory of Catrina in the snow.

When she insisted on standing upright, he refused to release her. "Alpha male. Say it!"

The amused twinkle in her eyes that had socked him in the solar plexus the previous evening reappeared. "Alpha male."

Satisfied, he removed his arms and reluctantly stepped away. "All right. You can go home to Titan now. I have a scene to write for tomorrow evening. Do you have a costume preference?"

"Surprise me."

He reflected on the clothing choices he'd unearthed in the walk-in closet. "Jenna played a scientist's assistant and love interest in that movie about an escaped genetic experiment that munched its way across Iowa."

Catrina wrinkled her nose. "A lab coat doesn't seem romantic to me."

"What about a role as an innocent virgin?"

She laughed outright, pleasing an aspect of his psyche walled up for a very long time. "Me as a virgin. Now *that's* a fantasy," she hooted. "Sure. Go for it. Write a scene about the seduction of a thirty-three-year-old virgin."

"I'll work on it," he promised.

"Goodnight." She made for her vehicle.

Feeling ridiculously protective—because *she* was the former cop, not to mention a security guard—Chett helped brush off the snow covering her vehicle while the engine warmed. Only when she drove out of the lot did he dig out of his pocket the keys to Jenna's SUV.

Catrina had requested a seduction scene. He tossed the keys lightly into the air and caught them in his thick glove, grinning. He actually looked forward to spending a few hours with his laptop instead of Johnnie Walker.

Progress.

CHAPTER 5

Dibs

At midafternoon, after completing the daily tour of her clients' properties, Catrina discovered a stuffed green garbage bag on the porch of her rented semidetached bungalow. She pulled a folded piece of computer paper from under the bag and opened it.

The note was brief:

Dinner will be at seven. As you will deduce from the costume, the time period is the 1870s. Please arrived dressed, without four-legged escort. Sorry, you can't read the script yet. You will have dialogue, mostly along the lines of "Yes, please." Chett

Smiling, Catrina unlocked the door, shed her parka, and filled Titan's bowls with kibble and fresh water while speculating about the bag's contents.

1870s, so a dance hall girl's saucy outfit? Maybe one of those exquisite low-cut off-the-shoulder gowns the women wore to balls? An image flashed of Chett kissing her bare shoulder in candlelight, then her neck, then her—

Restraining the eagerness that curled her toes inside her thermal socks, she nuked a cup of hot cocoa to warm her chilled fingers and insides. Finally, she sat at the kitchen table, with Titan flopped comfortably on the tile floor nearby, grabbed the green bag and pulled it between her knees.

Catrina plunged a hand into the bag and drew out a floor-length, midnight-blue woolen skirt with a bustle sewn in, a matching jacket, and a high-necked white blouse with tiny white cloth buttons running down the front and lace at the sleeve cuffs.

Catrina nibbled her bottom lip, a tad disappointed. *Hmmm. So* not *my idea of a provocative outfit.*

She couldn't recall a role in Jenna's early movies that required the sex siren to cover her assets so completely. Maybe she'd worn it for a bit part. On the other hand, given the risqué movies in which Jenna had starred prior to making it big, she had probably disrobed in a love scene. Or better yet, the hero had undressed her.

Okay, Catrina conceded. *This outfit has seduction possibilities.*

From deeper in the bag she retrieved a pair of soft white leather gloves, a round box containing a tiny felt hat with a feather plume and dangling ribbons to tie under the chin, and an uncomfortable-looking ivory corset with satin ribbons that laced up the back.

She held up the corset. "I'll never get this thing on by myself," she muttered to Titan. "I must call in reinforcements."

While waiting for Brigit to arrive, Catrina showered and struggled for half an hour to twist uncooperative hair into an updo. "No wonder they needed maids in those days," she grumbled to Titan. "It probably took hours to get a gentlewoman ready to step out of the bedroom."

Catrina had a glass of pinot noir poured and waiting when Brigit tapped on the front door after closing her tea shop at six.

"Come in," Catrina yelled from her bedroom.

Her friend let herself into the house on a blast of frigid air, her pert nose cherry red and peaking over a thick Hudson's Bay striped scarf covering her neck and mouth. "I had to walk. My car wouldn't start. Again."

She toed off winter boots, slung her parka over the back of an armchair, hung a shoulder bag on a hook out of Titan's reach, and unwound the scarf to expose a riot of blond curls framing her cherubic face. Ignoring the wine glass on a side table, Brigit made a beeline for the clothing Catrina had arranged on the navy sofa.

"Oooh," cooed Brigit, holding up the heavy floor-length skirt. "How fun. Too bad bustles aren't in fashion today. No one could tell how big my derrière is."

"Your butt is fine," Catrina called through the open bedroom door, the corset clutched to her naked torso. "Brigit, can you please lace me up?"

Brigit set the felt hat on her curls and trotted into the bedroom. In the dresser mirror she adjusted the angle of the hat feather, then to Catrina's reflection said, "You're so lucky to have a narrow waist. In those days I'd have needed *two* maids to squash me into a corset. On the other hand, I wouldn't have had to wear a bustle."

With the small hat perilously perched on her head, ribbons dangling, Brigit pressed her knee into Catrina's backside for leverage and grunted as she tugged the laces tight. "I sure wish *I'd* seen Chett first."

Catrina inhaled enough air into her compressed lungs to allow her to speak. "You have Brad."

"*That* guy." Brigit yanked especially hard on the laces.

"Ooof. Take it easy," Cat pleaded.

"All he cares about are his boat motors and winches and machine doohickeys," Brigit snorted, seriously miffed. "If I were a broken engine I'd get more attention."

"I thought you enjoyed your sex life."

"Mechanical," she seethed between gritted teeth as she pulled. "As in piston. In, out. In, out. Eject. The thrill of the drill is gone."

"Oh no! I thought you and Brad were getting along great. What happened?"

Brigit's dissatisfaction was news to Cat. Brad had a lot going for him: he ran a successful business, had an easy-going personality, and his swoon-worthy muscular body rated a ten. Therefore it was truly unfortunate he didn't turn Brigit's crank anymore. "Do you want to talk about it?"

Brigit tied the laces in a bow and took a break, breathing hard from the exertion. "That calls for wine."

She retrieved her wine glass and filled one for Catrina, then both women sank into the fluffy down comforter on the queen-sized bed and took healthy sips.

"You told me last summer that Brad is baby-daddy material," Catrina gently reminded Brigit. "Your biological clock is ticking, and you said you want kids."

Brigit cocked her head to one side. "Trade you Brad for Chett?"

Catrina didn't appreciate the predatory gleam in Brigit's round blue eyes. "Ha, ha. Seriously, what gives?"

Brigit drained her glass. "I'm bored," she admitted finally. "But here in Port Carson in the dead of winter, what choice do I have?"

Catrina had no answer to that one. The women's mutual problem, in a town with few eligible men in their age bracket, was finding a compatible local male partner. Cat had no interest in a long-term relationship. Or, to be honest, fear of subjecting a partner to the demons that bedeviled her kept Cat single. She therefore intended to enjoy a brief affair with Chett: no ties, no sleepovers, definitely no need for him to ever know she woke screaming most nights. Not even Brigit, her closest friend in Port Carson, knew *that* secret.

Brigit set her empty glass on the dresser, heaved a big sigh, then rallied. "You *must* have ringlets," she proclaimed. "Young ladies of that era wore their hair in masses of ringlets."

"At my age a virgin was called a spinster, not a young lady," Catrina replied dryly.

"You're twenty in this fantasy, so shut up about your age. He's older than you anyway."

After buttoning Catrina into the various articles of clothing, Brigit plugged in the curling iron, then selected bottles and tubes from Catrina's small assortment of makeup in the adjoining bathroom.

"I'm going to transform you into the loveliest virgin ever. Where's your perfume? Never mind, I'll use mine." She retrieved a vial from the depths of her shoulder bag.

"It's French and oh so alluring." She squirted the rose scent with a musky note behind Cat's ears, on the inside of her wrists, and between breasts plumped and bursting out of the top of the corset. "I'm experiencing this evening vicariously through you so I want details. I *insist* that you tell me every...single...thing he does to you," she begged as she stood on her toes to roll a swath of Catrina's hair onto the curling iron. "Bring home the script. Promise!"

Catrina laughed, then coughed. How on earth had women worn these constricting garments all day? She drew a shallow breath. "All right, I promise."

After fifteen minutes of wielding the curling iron like a pro, Brigit removed the hat from her head, placed it on Catrina's, tied the ribbons in a huge bow, then stood back to admire her efforts. "You look beautiful. He's gonna cast you in one of his movies, you gorgeous lady."

"If he casts me into his bed, I'll be happy with that." At the vision of their bodies entwined under crisp white sheets, Cat's knees weakened. She grasped the edge of the dresser with gloved hands. Swayed a little. "Brigit, please loosen the corset laces. No wonder women swooned at the drop of a handkerchief in those days."

As Brigit complied, she asked, "Were there any shoes in the bag?"

"No."

Cat considered her options. "I have some black patent leather ballet flats. They'll have to do."

Brigit finished tucking the blouse and jacket back into place, arranged the profusion of ringlets, then dug through her shoulder bag for her smartphone. "Before you go, let me take a picture. While you frolic the night away, Titan and I will withdraw to my parlor to watch the *Golden Globes* and eat leftover cupcakes from my shop."

At the sound of his name, Titan ambled over. Brigit stroked the soft fur under Titan's ears. "Sorry to get your hopes up, you big brute. No cupcakes for you."

Brigit zipped her parka while Catrina prepared to lock up. "Ask Chett if he's interested in writing a scene for three next time. And I don't mean Titan as the third in the ménage."

Catrina sucked in a shallow breath, clutched a gloved hand to her breast, and attempted to laugh off the outrageous request. *Share* Chett's attentions? Every cell in Catrina's body repelled the idea. She was equally shocked at the fierce possessiveness triggered by Brigit's request. Where had *that* come from?

"Since when did you become so adventurous?"

Brigit gathered her bag and Titan's leash. "Brad and I are over, although he doesn't know it yet. We haven't spent the night together since the hockey season started." Brigit confronted her friend directly. "Why not let me in on the fun?"

Cat struggled to form a response that wouldn't offend. She knew it would be dangerous to fall for the creative and interesting man from Hollywood. A crack in the protective guard she'd erected around her heart and soul might release a flood of emotions she couldn't control. At the same time she wanted Chett—his attention, fit physique, and fantasy scripts—to be exclusively hers and hers alone for the duration of his stay.

"Brigit," Cat said finally, staking her territory in what she hoped was a light and casual manner. "You're a darling friend, and I understand where the suggestion is coming from, but Chett is all mine until he gets on a plane to California!"

[♬ "Dibs"]

CHAPTER 6

The Seduction of Miss Prudence Maxwell

Catrina parked her vehicle on the leeside of Jenna's summer home, protecting the SUV from the bitter wind blowing streamers of snow off the frozen lake.

At her knock, Chett pulled open the heavy wood door. His dimpled delight at seeing her warmed her chilled insides faster than brandy. Clad in a crisp formal white shirt, thin black leather tie, black suit jacket and worn charcoal jeans, he looked like he'd stepped out of a *GQ* magazine photo. To suit the era, he'd slicked down neatly parted sun-streaked hair.

"You are exquisite," he said as he took her parka and winter boots and stowed them in Jenna's coat closet.

"Do I look good enough to eat?" She cocked her head of curls at him, deliberately provocative. His kissable lips beckoned, and she leaned in to touch hers to his lightly, then with more pressure as he deepened the kiss. A thrill swirled in her nether regions. She longed to be in his arms, naked, discovering what else those mobile lips could do to her.

"Patience," he chuckled, pulling away. "I'm preparing lake trout for dinner."

She didn't care about the meal. She'd comply and let him feed her first, but only because they'd both need to stoke their energy for the night ahead.

Shaking the ballet flats out of a drawstring cloth shoe bag, she removed her thick wool socks to slide bare feet into the shoes, then followed Chett into the great room. Drafts ruffled the flames of stubby white candles in glass holders on the fireplace mantle, on the round table in the dining nook set for two, and on every flat surface in the room. Green-tipped flames leaped in the wood-burning fireplace. Enchanting fluttering light gilded the space, not quite reaching shadowed corners.

"There was no electricity in Virginia City, California in the 1880s," Chett explained as he handed her a glass of chilled Chardonnay.

"Virginia City? The setting for tonight, I presume." She sipped the wine and held the cool glass to one cheek. "My, it's warm in here."

"Your comfort means everything to me." He lifted her free hand and pressed the back to his lips. Her heartbeat quickened as cocky blue eyes met hers. "Big Joe Grifter, ma'am, at your service. Itinerant gambler, rustler, and all around rake."

She pressed a gloved hand to her heart in a decorous pretend swoon. Deep within, her blood heated. *Ohhhh, a bad boy.* "And I am—?"

"Until today your name was Miss Prudence Maxwell, innocent daughter of an impecunious gentleman who regrettably fares poorly at poker."

"My father's broke."

"Not only that, in his most recent game he bet his daughter's hand in marriage. And lost. Or rather, it was *my* lucky night at the card table."

Catrina sipped her wine. The cool liquid slid down a throat dry with anticipation. "Ahhh. I expect I am not terribly keen on becoming the wife of a stranger who is patently a blackguard."

"Precisely, my dear Prudence. However you no longer have the option to refuse me. Despite tears and protestations on your part, your papa dragged you to the preacher this afternoon and we were married to pay the considerable debt. Tonight is our, ah, wedding night."

He raised his glass to her in salute. A self-satisfied grin curled the corners of his mouth. It was the smile of a man who'd won the girl and was primed to enjoy the spoils. The arrogant sexual confidence he wore like James Bond had nothing to do with the part he was supposedly playing.

Inwardly she sighed. Ethically and as a modern woman Catrina took issue with patriarchy and forced marriage. Chett's scene concept was yet another lopsided male fantasy. What else could she expect from a man who wrote screenplays for adolescent male audiences? Nevertheless, she'd have a difficult time pretending to resist the advances of this handsome new "husband" of hers. She narrowed her eyes as a plan formed. Thinking fast on her feet was her forte. "May I read the script?"

"Naturally." He handed her a few sheets of paper and returned to the kitchen to check on the meal. She placed her wine glass and script on the coffee table and arranged the bulky skirt so she could sit gracefully on the white leather sofa.

While he gathered dinner plates and cutlery, she scanned the typed pages. It only took a minute. She turned them over. Blank. A seduction scene was nowhere to be found. "The dialogue ends right after dessert." She tried but failed to keep disappointment out of her tone.

"You taught me to believe in improvisation," Chett replied from the other side of the kitchen island. "If at any time you draw a blank, the words *more* and *again* are useful."

Her lips twitched and she lay the script down. A delightful craving for what was to come squelched her hunger. The tight corset left little room in her stomach for food anyway. The sooner Big Joe and Prudence dispensed with the preliminaries, the better.

She rose and minced over to the kitchen, the full skirt swishing against her bare legs. A lemony aroma wafted from the narrow covered pan poaching the trout on the stovetop. "Can I help?"

"The food's ready. Our appetizer is salad." From the refrigerator Chett removed a salad bowl, placed tongs crosswise on top, and handed it to her. "Have a seat, wife, and I'll be right over."

She carried the salad to the round table banked on three sides by floor-to-ceiling windows that, in daylight, gave diners a panoramic view of the lake. On the floor beside the table, a bottle of champagne cooled in a rustic metal bucket filled with snow.

The window glazing reflected the candlelight like a mirror. For a heartbeat, Catrina's reflection—the image of a beautiful slender woman in a plumed hat, her eyes aglow, full lips parted—shimmered out of time against the inky backdrop of a moonless night.

"A bride on her wedding night," she murmured. *I sure wish that could be me in real life.* Her biological clock was ticking, just like Brigit's. However, Catrina had squelched her own desire for marriage and children. The relentless, draining fallout from debilitating nightmares left her emotionally fragile, and all her energy was devoted to keeping herself together, with none left over for maintaining a long term relationship, let alone raising a tiny, dependent human.

She breathed in, instructing herself to ignore her grim reality in order to focus on the fun here and now—the fantasy seduction that Chett had planned. She undid the pearl button on the inside wrist of each leather glove, tugged at tense fingers, and placed her gloves and feathered hat between the dripping wax candles in artisan blown-glass bowls on the antique pine sideboard.

As she was about to sit at the linen-draped table, Big Joe arrived to hold an antique oak Windsor chair for her. She arranged her skirt and sat primly in character, hands folded on her lap. From an inside jacket pocket he unfolded his script and propped it upright against a vase of carnations so they could both read it.

"Champagne?"

Catrina spoke quickly, betraying nervous excitement. "Did they even have champagne in Virginia City back then?"

"Imported from France, carried by steamship to New York City and transported by transcontinental railroad to San Francisco." Chett lifted the bottle from the bucket, dried it with a striped cotton dishcloth, and poured the champagne into flutes.

Tonight she sensed a playful lightness in Chett's demeanor. Gone was the fierce anger that had so unnerved her when they first met. Cat sipped the effervescent liquid. "Champagne must have been as precious as gold in those days."

"The California Gold Rush was over by 1855. California became a state in 1850." He lowered his tight butt into the chair across from her. Adorable dimples bookended his grin.

Catrina tilted her head thoughtfully, onto him. *He's procrastinating with me instead of working.* "Obviously you did quite a bit of research for this scenario."

He ignored the sly dig and raised his glass. "To my lovely bride." With a jerk of his head he indicated the script.

She obediently slid her gaze away from his handsome features rendered Peter Pan youthful in the candlelight in order to read and speak her lines. "I shall obtain an annulment," she retorted in character. "Surely the judge will not refuse my request under the circumstances. I agreed to marry you only to keep my father out of debtors' prison."

"The circuit judge is not due in Virginia City for weeks. I portend that you will have abandoned the pursuit of an amendment by the time he arrives."

"Nothing will change my mind." She heaped salad on her side plate and lifted a forkful of the leafy greens tossed with artichoke hearts, feta cheese, and a touch of vinaigrette dressing. *Delicious.* Perhaps the meal was a good idea after all.

Big Joe speared an artichoke on the end of his fork and waved it. "In the interim you will pass many nights in my bed, my dear wife. Your virtue will be compromised."

She finished her salad and lay down her fork to read her lines. "I must save myself for my true love." With spirit, she proclaimed, "You are ostensibly my husband only due to a coerced signature on the record of marriage. I did not vow to love, honor, and obey. *Especially* obey." She nodded, agreeing with that last statement at least. *Did any woman vow to obey her husband anymore?*

Big Joe rose to remove their empty salad plates. "As your husband I have rights. I intend to exercise those rights by the end of the evening with your willing participation."

His expression radiated desire and sexual confidence. Anticipation of promised pleasure shivered down Cat's spine. Each sip of expensive French champagne and line of dialogue had blurred the fine line between reality and fantasy. In the moment she identified with Prudence, a woman perilously attracted despite knowing it was folly to fall in love with a man so unsuitable. *Be careful,* warned a part of her buried deep.

Chett returned with the main course on Jenna's white china, and set a filled plate before Catrina.

"This looks wonderful." She smiled up at him. "So you can cook, among all your other talents."

Chett waggled his eyebrows. "I have yet another talent for you to discover."

Over lemon-garnished trout, baked potatoes, and steamed vegetables, they bantered. "Tell me, Prudence, have you ever kissed a man?"

"I have been courted."

Chett leaned across the table, a ploy to focus her attention on him instead of the food. "That's not what I asked, wife. Has a man clasped you in his arms and tasted those rosebud lips in a passionate embrace that heated your blood?"

Warmth coursed above the stiff collar of her blouse, his words like fuel on the simmering desire that had overridden all logic the previous two days. The next line in the script directed her to assure her new husband of her virginal inexperience. *Ha.* He'd given her the perfect opening to flip the dynamic.

Prudence lowered her fork and improvised. "I have experienced passion," she admitted with a coy tilt of her head. She sensuously cupped a palm over her left breast plumped high by the corset. "I have imagined the touch of a man's hand on my bosom."

Big Joe's gaze fastened on the languorous brush of her finger across the mound in parallel with the glide of the tip of her tongue across her bottom lip. He swallowed, both hands gripping the edge of the table. "A proper woman such has yourself has never—"

She arched her breasts forward, a coquette in demure clothing. "I confess, Big Joe, that in my dreams men come to me late at night when I am alone in my bed. On occasion *two* strong, virile men have...pleasured me simultaneously far into the night." She tilted her chin up to the ceiling, drew sensuous fingers down the line of her neck, and said with feigned regret, "Married women tell me to expect disappointment on my wedding night. I despair because a real man can never be as skilled in the art of pleasuring a woman."

Big Joe cleared his throat, pushed back his chair and jumped to his feet. "I promise you that *this* real man has the skills." He strode around the table to pull her up into his arms. As he lowered his lips to hers, he whispered, "You can't wait, can you? I do admire a woman who goes after what she wants."

Their kiss sparked a spiral of intense need that had her wrapping her arms around his torso and angling her pelvis at the bulge in his pants.

He stripped off her jacket and flung it over the back of the dining chair. After a brief interlude of groping hands and feathery kisses under her ear, the skirt joined its mate. His fingers fumbled with the tiny buttons on her blouse.

"Allow me," Prudence insisted.

While her eager fingers flicked open the blouse buttons, Chett picked up a remote control from the sideboard and pressed. A crooning voice flowed from hidden speakers.

[♬ "Sexuality"]

"k. d. lang's hit *Sexuality* seems the ideal accompaniment for, ah, dessert." Chett tugged the blouse sleeves from her arms, murmuring the sensuous lyrics he'd memorized.

Clad only in the corset, a pair of lace panties, and her ballet flats, Prudence was conscious of his attention fixed on the mounds of white breasts spilling over the crest of the hourglass undergarment.

He bent to kiss one breast, then the other. "Beautiful. You...are...beautiful." Each word was a soft caress.

He drew her over to the warmth of the fireplace, snagged a split log from the basket at the edge of the hearth and tossed it onto red-hot logs crumbling in the iron grate. She kicked off her ballet flats and wiggled her toes into the thick, soft faux lambskin rugs that he'd layered on the hearth rug. He'd thought of every detail.

No longer smiling, he placed his hands on her cinched waist. Firelight flickered over features strained with banked desire. He wanted her, perhaps even more than she wanted him. No man had ever gazed upon her with such appreciation. Such anticipation. Reflected in his eyes she intuited how he viewed her—achingly lovely, an undiscovered pleasure. There is only ever one first time, and he'd created the circumstances to make it special for both of them.

"Shall I demonstrate how Big Joe would seduce his virgin bride?"

"Yes, please."

Flashing resistance-is-futile dimples, he shed his jacket and tie. Facing her once again, he hooked his thumbs over the edge of her panties and pulled them down while lightly trailing his long fingers to explore her backside, thighs and calves. Rising to his full height, he wrapped his left arm around her waist and pulled her to his hard chest. His mouth descended on hers, warm breath hinting of champagne and leashed lust.

They kissed, lost in each other. Her arms crept up his back, the better to hold herself upright.

His forefinger found her moist bud. She stiffened in surprise. He buried his face between her soft white breasts, his soft lips tasting, nibbling, until she relaxed. Then his finger began to move. Slowly. Expertly. Smoothly. In time with the insistent song lyrics that urged her to let go.

His tongue dipped below the corset to encircle one nipple, flooding her with an overwhelming sensation. She moaned and tried to squirm to adjust the pressure but he held her too tightly. She was so close. So exquisitely close. She clutched the cotton fabric of his shirt with desperate fingers. Only his strong arms kept her from sinking boneless to the floor.

His forefinger slipped inside, and his thumb replaced it to rub the slippery throbbing tip. His finger curved inside and expertly slid over the wet sensitive surface. Time stopped as sensation layered upon sensation.

Until she toppled over the edge. Her entire body shuddered in his arms. "Big Joe," she cried.

He locked his lips to hers while the ripples of her electric release flooded her nerves down to her toes.

Slowly he lowered her to the soft furs and began to remove his pants and unbutton his shirt. "Do you ride, Prudence?" he asked incongruously.

She gathered wits floating like the rest of her body. "Obviously a girl in the old west would be able to ride."

"Ride me." He lay beside her across the length of the hearth, naked and erect with a condom already in place.

She swung a leg over his golden skin gleaming in the firelight. He had no tan line, she noted, as she encircled his long engorged member with one hand to guide it home.

"Big Joe is an appropriate handle," she teased, then bit her bottom lip as he filled her. "O.M.G."

"Too big?" he asked, concerned.

What an ego. She tossed her head back to laugh. Then he shifted his hips and she lost track of her thoughts. "I'm extraordinarily sensitive in there," she breathed. "I think I'm coming again. Or still coming. Oh—Chett, take me quick."

He flipped her onto her back and supported his weight with one muscled arm. With three thrusts he finished, tumbling them both into mutual gasping release.

***

Two hours of love-making later, Catrina was cozily embraced in Chett's arms and spooned against his muscular heat on the faux furs in front of the fireplace. Her eyelids felt so heavy. She opened them wide, telling herself that she absolutely needed to get up and go home before sleep enveloped her. It was imperative.

But she felt so warm. His body tucked against hers felt so *wonderful*. One more minute of bliss and then she'd leave...

Exhaustion tipped her over the edge into sleep.

Hours or maybe only minutes later, the tenacious nightmare slithered from its lair and took control of her subconscious, replaying the dive that had broken her mind, her life. At the inky, cold depth of one hundred eighty feet underwater, a dozen pairs of glassy dead eyes reflected the light of her headlamp.

Catrina jerked awake, a fist already in her mouth to stifle a scream, oblivious to the sharp pain of her teeth sunk deep into scarred fingers. The horror paralyzed her limbs as effectively as during the actual incident. Adrenaline gushed into her bloodstream. Her frozen heart battered against its cage of ribs, imprisoned like the dead women in their watery dungeon.

No one knew about the nightmare that inevitably claimed her night after long night.

No one knew that Titan nudged her flailing arms when, immersed in the nightmare, she frantically tried to swim away from those crystal eyes. Titan brought her back to reality by nosing her wet cheeks. If that did not work, he barked.

Titan rescued her, night after night. *I need my dog.*

Chett stirred and pulled her tight to his warm, solid chest. His voice drowsy, he murmured, "Sleep, my Cat."

Agitated, Catrina tore his hand from her breast and flung his arm from around her waist. "I have to go."

Chett levered up on an elbow, his naked torso red gold in the light from fireplace embers. "The powder room is down the hall to the left."

She scrambled to her feet. "I have to go *home*. Titan needs me," she said, omitting the fact that the dog was staying overnight at Brigit's apartment.

"Cat, it's freezing outside. It must be after midnight. Titan will be fine until morning," he said reasonably.

Reason had nothing to do with her need to escape. "I can't do this." *That much is true.*

"You can't stay overnight?" He rubbed his eyes.

"No." Catrina inhaled deeply to control the trembling in her voice. "I can't be in a relationship after all. We're done."

[♬ "Little Man"]

CHAPTER 7

Catrina Turns Tail

She was leaving? Chett scrambled to his feet. "I thought you had fun tonight."

"I did," Catrina mumbled in a monotone stripped of the passion that had consumed them for hours.

He ran both hands over his head to clear the sleep that fogged his understanding of what the hell was happening. "Cat, what's wrong?"

"Thank you for dinner. For everything." Bare-assed, ribbons trailing from the corset she clutched to her breasts, she stumbled over to the closet, pulled out her parka and shoved her arms into the sleeves.

As Catrina reached for the door latch, Chett flicked on a side table lamp. The light startled her. Her gaze skittered in his direction, her eyes black holes punched in a blanched, wary face, an animal seeking escape. What had happened during the few hours they'd slept to make her act this way? He'd no clue. "What can I do? Tell me."

"I made a mistake."

Second thoughts. The excuse joined other barbs stacked in a frozen corner of his soul. Cat was definitely not the first woman to bail when she'd taken what she wanted from him. Crushed, he said only, "You've forgotten your boots."

Confused, she looked down at her bare feet, then around the foyer, at a loss as to where he'd stowed her bulky Arctic-grade boots. She waited dismally until Chett wrapped his jeans around his bare middle against the chill and hurried over.

He opened the closet door wide to locate her boots beside his on the drip tray, and set them before her. "Do you have your keys?"

"They're in the SUV." She shoved her feet into the boots without fastening them, and yanked open the heavy front door, face averted. Frigid air swept into the room. "Goodbye, Chett," she said, head averted. "Sorry."

Chett felt the bottom of his world sink deeper into the purgatory of his existence for the past year: no wife, no work, no income. A pathetic plea escaped. "Tell me and I'll fix it."

She faced him at last, her inscrutable dark eyes glistening in the light reflected from the lamp. "This"—she threw an arm out in a wide gesture that encompassed the great room and him—"is not working for me. You'll…you'll have better luck with my friend Brigit," Cat choked. "She wants you bad." She stepped out into the icy wind and pulled the heavy door closed behind her, not waiting to hear Chett's reply.

"I want *you* bad," he said to the empty house. Chett yanked opened the door, welcomed the glacial air that numbed his emotions, and waited for the cold engine of the SUV to turn over. He watched as she made a three-point turn, the beams of the headlights bouncing off flakes of thickly falling snow, and gunned the engine. The SUV raced up the slope.

After her vehicle turned onto the road at the top of the lane, he slammed and locked the door, then gathered up his clothes and dressed. The half-empty forty ouncer on the sideboard beckoned, but he ignored it. For once, instead of using alcohol to suppress reminders of his failures as a lover, husband, and screenwriter, he *wanted* to keep his brain sharp.

He threw a couple of logs on the fire, thoughtful. Facts were facts. Catrina patently enjoyed the evening and the lovemaking. He knew actresses, and Catrina's exuberant passion was no act. Everything was fine—rather wonderful, actually—until she had fallen asleep. He wanted to think about her no-overnight rule, what might have spooked her, why she ran.

Cat's good for me. I need to step up and figure out how to be good for her.

***

"For a woman who supposedly enjoyed a night of passion, you look miserable." Brigit placed a mug filled with hot coffee laced with cream on a coaster on the vintage mahogany coffee table in front of Catrina. "Where's the post-coital glow, girl?"

At ten o'clock on a grey Monday morning, the SereniTea Shoppe's half dozen round tables were empty except for two elderly ladies gossiping over a pot of tea, scones and homemade jam beside the bow window overlooking Main Street.

At the back of the room, out of earshot, Brigit had pulled two armchairs slipcovered in spring green and white chintz close to a small gas fireplace with an antique carved walnut mantle. It threw off enough heat to displace chilly drafts from the French doors that opened to a rear balcony overlooking Lake Muskoka.

On either side of the fireplace, bookcases held Brigit's collection of cozy mystery novels with food themes. She insisted she bought the paperbacks for the recipes. Indeed, the glass display cases by the cash register tempted tourists and locals with an ever-changing variety of tarts, pies, cookies, cupcakes, breads, and scones. Brigit loved to bake.

Brigit placed two plates, napkins, and a tiered cupcake stand on the coffee table within easy reach and sank into soft cushions opposite Catrina.

From the enticing selection, Cat chose an angel food cupcake topped with a swirl of mint buttercream icing and rainbow sprinkles.

"The evening didn't turn out quite the way I expected," Catrina mumbled around a mouthful of cake. She slid her tongue across her upper lip to dislodge the sugary confection. "I don't want to talk about it."

Brigit eyed her over the rim of her mug of peppermint tea. "He's a disappointment, eh?"

Catrina reached for a chocolate cupcake with mocha icing adorned with chocolate chips and placed it on her plate. *It's a two-cupcake kinda day.* "You want him? You can have him. We're done."

"But if the sex was awful, why would I—"

Catrina's heart lurched. *Awful? Hardly.* They'd gone at each other like rabbits until she lost consciousness from exhaustion. "His...equipment works fine. That's not the reason. We're not compatible, that's all. Satisfied?"

"Not compatible, how?" Brigit pressed.

Catrina reached for a third cupcake while her sleep-deprived brain struggled to invent an answer that would satisfy her friend.

Brigit widened her sky-blue eyes and raised blond brows in exaggerated shock. "You're such a health nut, you never eat *three* cupcakes! You must be *really* upset."

"He pushed my buttons," Cat said finally. It was close enough to the truth. The previous night's fun and games had triggered a powerful nightmare that was even more emotionally charged than usual. It had terrified her. No, worse. She'd been on the precipice of a full blown anxiety attack and she was desperate to avoid a repeat. Unfortunately she'd developed a crush on the guy. That was the heart of the problem. It wasn't Chett's fault that lust lifted the lid on dark emotions she struggled daily to control. Staying far, far away solved the problem.

"He's not for me," she lied. "I'm moving on."

Given the lack of available men in Port Carson, Brigit kindly refrained from adding the obvious "to whom." Instead she changed the subject. "I watched the *Golden Globes* last night. Jenna Jordan didn't win."

Cat set the half-eaten third cupcake on her plate and sipped her cooling coffee while she digested the news. "Then Jenna is sure to ramp up pressure on Chett to finish a screenplay for her. That's another good excuse for me to keep out of his way. So he can work."

"You told me the playacting was helping him develop ideas." Brigit shot her a considered look. "Maybe *I'll* invite Chett to the Port Carson Winter Carnival next weekend."

"Be my guest." Catrina reached for the unfinished cupcake, then withdrew her hand when a stab of pain cramped her stomach. Funny, Brigit's delicious baking had never affected her this way before.

Brigit leaned forward to peer into Cat's face. "Eyes are windows to the soul, and yours are tearing up. I don't think you mean it. I do believe Chett's gotten under your skin. You're falling for him. As in falling in *love*."

Catrina scoffed. "No way. We just met." Last night Chett's sensitive, expert lovemaking had relaxed her, lowered her guard. She'd accidentally dozed off. It must never happen again. "It's over. I can't be with him," she insisted, her insides twisting.

"If you're sure."

"Positive." If Chett took up with Brigit, then Catrina couldn't be tempted. Win-win. "He's all yours."

Brigit settled back into the cushions, her round features bright with eagerness. "Then I should drop by and welcome Chett to Muskoka. I wonder if he prefers pie or cookies?"

Catrina lurched to her feet. "I need to use your restroom." To be sick.

CHAPTER 8

Mirror, Mirror on the Wall

"I'm counting on you, darling." Jenna's voice was pitched high with the effects of a pharmaceutical.

Chett winced.

After the Golden Globe Award for Best Performance by an Actress in a Supporting Role went to a stacked young thing barely out of puberty instead of to Jenna, she didn't even wait until she recovered from a killer hangover to contact Chett. It didn't take a genius to figure out why. She needed him to come through for her. Unfortunately the pages he'd written to that point were intended for another performer, and the "action" involved seduction. *Lust in Space* wasn't going to cut it with Jenna.

Chett tossed out a logline off the top of his head. "A mob hitman meets his match when he's ordered to kill a female assassin."

"It's been *done*, Chett. *Mr. & Mrs. Smith*, for gawd's sake! And the mafia again. Really?" Her voice tightened. "I want something *fresh* to pitch to producers and studio executives at a party next Saturday night."

Fresh, huh. He had nothing. Chett felt the screws tighten. "Studios buy scripts similar to those of successful films," he reminded her. "*Mafia Massacre* was big. *Mr. & Mrs. Smith* was big."

"Yeah, years ago." Jenna's tone dripped with aggrieved frustration. "Ancient history. Move on."

For a few minutes they discussed recent dramas that had been nominated for, or had won, awards for best screenplay and best picture. Given Jenna hadn't won an acting award, ever, neither needed to mention that a blockbuster budget and a mature male A-list actor like Robert Downey, Jr., Tom Cruise or George Clooney were no longer in the cards. An action spec script packaged with international distribution agreements was their best chance to entice a studio to greenlight a $50 million film starring Jenna Jordan.

"I want a new concept by Wednesday." Jenna's order cut across the continent like a fencer's thrust, laying bare the steely resolve that gave rise to career longevity in an unforgiving industry that broke many young actors' hearts. "Send me a logline and a three-page synopsis outlining the key scenes. Don't even begin to write the treatment until I vet the concept." She sighed, paused, and regrouped. "Meanwhile, my manager has a call out for spec scripts."

Her words sank into dead air as Chett's heart slammed against his ribs. When he could again speak calmly, he pried apart gritted teeth and growled, "We have a deal."

"Darling," she said, her voice artificially bright, "you get that I *must* have something to pitch next Saturday, right? So send me something I love."

His shoulders sagged. He wasn't going to win this debate. "Will do." Bottom line, Chett had forty-eight hours to beat out the competition with a better idea, or she'd run with a finished screenplay. He ran his fingers through his hair and stared dismally at the strands entwined in his fingers. "Anything else?"

"I'm rail thin after dieting to fit into my Golden Globes gown. I look fantastic in a bikini. Consider locations in Florida or The Bahamas."

"Sure, Jenna." He peered out the frosty great room window past the icicles and down to the frozen snow-covered lake. He swiped a hand across his eyes. "And thanks for the use of your lake house. I can't think of a better place to write your screenplay set in Florida."

[♬ "Kokomo"]

***

Late Monday afternoon, as the sun began its descent, Catrina braked the SUV at the entrance to Jenna's lane. Cat's duty to complete the last stop on her rounds warred with stomach-churning reluctance to encounter Chett. Beside her, Titan woofed softly and pawed at the passenger-side door, eager to exit and sniff animal tracks in the woods. At the bottom of the plowed laneway, smoke curled from the chimney into clear cold air. Chett was at home. She shouldn't disturb him, she told herself. He'd call her if anything went wrong at the lake house.

She conveniently ignored the fact he'd left two voicemails and three texts on her cell phone that day. They were "how are you?" calls. Nothing that required a response, she told herself.

Titan's ears narrowed into forward points, and a low whine escaped his throat. He'd alerted to a scent. Cat scanned the snowbanks on both sides of the road but saw nothing. Then her eye caught a blur as a white fur ball separated from the snow and bounded into the forest. The message wasn't lost on Catrina. Turning tail and running away like a scared rabbit, that was her. She'd run from the police force, run from well-meaning friends in the big city.

She had nowhere left to run.

She didn't want to drive down that lane. She didn't want to put on snowshoes and tramp a circuit of the property to verify all was secure. Most of all, she didn't want to have to face Chett in order to return the corset and empty hatbox in a plastic bag on the vehicle's back seat.

It's closure, she told herself. *I won't have to see him ever again.* Anxiety that she'd cave and throw herself into his arms tightened her gut, forcing acid from a stomach filled with four cups of coffee into her esophagus. She breathed deep. Then again.

The force is strong in him, she thought, paraphrasing an iconic line in the *Star Wars* movie. *Do I have the strength to resist this attraction?*

You have no choice, she answered herself. *Keep this up and the freakish emotions you hold at bay are gonna be unleashed. They'll erupt in public, and that'll be the end of living in Port Carson.* She breathed. *Chett will fly home to Hollywood soon. Then everything will return to normal.*

Her dull daily routine. No fun. No sex. No costumes. She shook her head to banish this dismal future, then put the vehicle in gear. *I'll drop the stuff off and skedaddle.*

After parking beside the garage and turning off the engine, Catrina retrieved the bag from the back seat and quick-stepped across the driveway to the house. She was about to sling the handles of the plastic bag over the door-knob when, to her chagrin, Chett opened the door.

"Cat?" Her name on his exhale fogged in the frigid air. "How are you?"

Against her will, her heart thudded faster under the heavy parka. Chett looked ruggedly adorable in a T-shirt, jeans, tousled sun-bleached hair, and bare feet. She sucked in air cold enough to stiffen her backbone. *I can do this.* She nodded in greeting. "Fine." She handed him the bag.

"What's this?"

"The corset. From the costume."

"Oh, right. Come on in. I made a fresh pot of coffee."

She took a step back. "No time, sorry. I have to finish my rounds."

His dubious expression disputed her pitiful end-of-day

excuse, but he was too polite to say so out loud. He countered with a request. "Would you do me a big favor? I'm in the middle of something urgent for Jenna. Can you collect the various articles of clothing and tell me if any of them need to be dry-cleaned? If not, could you put them all back in the garment bag in Jenna's closet for me?" He shrugged with unconscious charm. "Women's clothing. I'm at a loss."

Forgetting that she wanted to avoid him, that she never wanted to be with him again, dismay froze her boots to the shoveled concrete stoop. *What about last night,* she wanted to scream. *Didn't it mean anything to you?*

Chett stamped his bare feet in the open doorway. "This cold is freezing my nuts. What do you say?"

She was about to turn down his reasonable request, then paused. Some instinct alerted her to an opportunity the way Titan alerted to a wild creature. Professional ethics prevented Cat from snooping through the closets and drawers in her clients' vacation homes, but now Chett was offering access to Jenna's costume collection. An offer no woman worthy of the gender could refuse. This was her last chance before Brigit claimed Chett.

Cat bit her bottom lip, torn. All those movie costumes in her size...the heady, hot, heightened sensations as Chett eyed her wearing the skintight lizard costume and smutty low-cut corset...

Sampling Jenna's collection had left Cat eager to explore it more fully. She teetered on the edge of agreeing. "You're busy?"

"Yeah." He retreated to give her space to enter. "I'm on a deadline."

He seemed twitchy. Stressed. Sincere. So no attempts to seduce her then. She trembled with relief. Or was it disappointment?

"I'll do it." She stepped into the foyer.

Chett closed the door behind her and waved at the blouse and skirt that "Miss Prudence" had tossed on a chair while being undressed by her husband, "Big Joe" the previous evening. "I haven't had a chance to tidy up. Jenna called," he explained vaguely.

Catrina toed off her boots and hung her parka in the closet. "I'll be out of here inside ten minutes. I can't leave Titan in the SUV for long."

He stayed her with a gentle hand on her forearm and peered into her face. "Are you okay? Did you sleep?"

Tears unexpectedly welled in her eyes. She angled her chin away from his scrutiny, her jaw clamped tight.

"We need to talk," he urged. When Catrina shook her head, mute, he added, "When you're ready."

I'll never be ready. Catrina took the plastic bag from him and hurried around the room to scoop up clothing, hat and gloves.

"The closet is in the second bedroom on the left," Chett called as she bounded up the stairs.

In a guest room that overlooked the garage behind the house, Catrina entered the adjacent walk-in closet and whistled. *Some closet!* Clear plastic garment bags hung from rods on three sides of a large dressing room. In the center of the space, an empty garment bag and hangers lay across a square upholstered bench. A three-sided full-length mirror and the door occupied the fourth side of the room.

She pushed a few labeled garment bags along a section of rod to see how the other costumes had been arranged inside the bags, then similarly hung the skirt, jacket, and corset. She tucked the hatbox and gloves into the garment bag's bottom zipped compartment for accessories. The blouse she set aside to be professionally cleaned and pressed.

Satisfied that Jenna would not notice anything out of order, Catrina surveyed the array of brightly colored costumes. With Titan waiting in the vehicle, she only had a few more minutes. Apple green satin fabric called to her, and she extracted a garment bag containing a ball gown. The label indicated Jenna had worn it as an extra in a Regency-era ballroom scene.

What the heck. It'll only take a minute.

She carefully removed the exquisite gown from the bag, ran a finger over delicate ivory lace at the neck and sleeves, and held the empire-waist skirt and low-cut bodice against her figure in front of the mirror. She swayed, imagining Chett attired in a black wool fitted tailcoat and white cravat like a blond Colin Firth in the TV miniseries *Pride and Prejudice*.

Chett would bow, take her hand, and escort her onto the dance floor. His eyes would drift from her eyes to her mouth to the soft mounds rising from her bodice. His breath would quicken. He'd pull her close to conceal from other dancers the bulge straining against the buttons of his tight breeches. Straining to be one with her...

No. It will never happen again.

Catrina carefully returned the gown to its protective sheath and pushed aside other garment bags to make room for it on the nearest rod. She itched to examine every costume. There must be three dozen in total. She checked her watch and figured she had several more minutes before the interior of her vehicle cooled to a temperature uncomfortable for Titan.

Swiftly she slid garment bags—labeled with Jenna's name, type of costume, scene and movie title—along the nearest rod one by one: a harem costume; the scientist's lab coat Chett had mentioned, complete with fake security badge on a lanyard in the accessory pouch; a tube top, mini skirt, thigh-high boots and shoulder bag in a bag labeled *Prostitute*; a pink feathered bra, panties, and feathered headpiece with rhinestones in a bag labeled *Showgirl Chorus*; an off-shoulder peasant gown labeled *Pirate Wench*; a silvery-blue gown and ermine-trimmed velvet cape, hat and muff labeled *Lady-in-Waiting*; and a gold-sequined strapless gown and matching heels in a bag tagged *Nightclub Singer*.

She extracted the showgirl bag for a closer look because the costume reminded her of a favorite film, *Chicago*, starring Renée Zellweger and Catherine Zeta-Jones. She posed in front of the mirror, feathered bra against her breasts, hip cocked, lips pursed coquettishly. The image sparked daringly naughty thoughts that triggered a tingling desire for Chett to see her in the skimpy feathered bra and high-cut panties. Her skin heated, traitorously threatening to melt her willpower.

No. I must not sleep with him again.

When she reluctantly returned the outfit to the rack, she pushed aside the adjacent garment bag to make space. Inside it, a navy cop uniform, complete with badge and handcuffs, arrested her heart. She gasped, imprisoning air in paralyzed lungs.

Jenna's closet faded to murk.

Catrina found herself in the women's locker room at the Toronto Police Marine Unit, her uniformed self reflected in a cracked mirror. Next door in the temporary morgue, a dozen zipped plastic body bags awaited body removal vans.

"No!" She clutched her traitorous brain between shaking palms. Racking, rasping sobs shook her frame, shook loose the sickening image from the shift that ended her career. *My flashbacks never happen when I'm awake. What the hell is happening to me?*

But the scene in her mind's eye bizarrely dissolved to fresh hell. Garment bags containing beautiful fabrics, feathers, and rhinestones morphed into grey body bags stuffed with dead teenage girls in wet rags.

Catrina squeezed her eyes shut in a futile effort to block the vision. Her knees gelled and she collapsed. Her lungs screamed for air, like in a dive gone wrong. Her horrified heart hammered loud enough, fast enough, to wake the drowned. *Boom-boom-boom-boom-boom...*

Suddenly strong arms lifted her, clutched her to a warm, *live* body.

"Catrina, what's wrong?" Chett's faint voice penetrated the whooshing in her ears.

She buried her face against his chest, her lungs straining to absorb a breath, and another, on which to float out the words "I don't...want to be...held hostage by my past... anymore."

CHAPTER 9

Ruff Day

"Cat, you're hyperventilating. Take deep, slow breaths." Chett dragged Catrina's limp body over to the upholstered bench and propped her against it, her long legs splayed out in front.

He recognized a panic attack from his fear-of-dogs experiences. He crouched beside her, took a few deep breaths of his own, and ordered his mind to produce options.

Call 911.

But his phone was downstairs on the kitchen counter, and he refused to leave Cat alone while she struggled for air. He had to increase the level of carbon dioxide in her blood, and fast, before her brain starved of oxygen and she lost consciousness.

He reached for the discarded plastic bag on the bench. It wasn't a paper bag, but it would have to do. He rolled down the top handles, compressed the round opening in a fist, and blew into the bag, inflating it. He then quickly placed the top over her nose and mouth. "Breath out, then in."

To his relief, she obeyed. Even in the throes of panic she must've recalled her first aid training. He inflated the bag with a long exhale, and demanded, "Again. Out, in, out."

Five minutes later her lungs filled and emptied in a normal rhythm. He relaxed, slumped from his knees to sit on the floor beside her, and pulled her head onto his chest.

"I would have preferred mouth-to-mouth," she mumbled against his T-shirt.

Still shaken—no, make that *scared*—for her, he forced a chuckle. If she could joke, she must be okay. He tipped her chin up and dropped a light kiss on her cool lips. "You had me worried."

"Titan!" She pressed a palm on Chett's chest to lever herself upright.

"You're not going anywhere," he growled, covering her hand with his. "You need recovery time. Food. Something to drink."

She ignored him, sat up, then stood. "I have to bring him inside. The temperature's dropping." She pressed a hand to one temple and swayed alarmingly. "The goddamn closet is spinning."

He scrambled to his feet and stabilized her shivering shoulders. "You're in no condition to go outside." He swallowed. Manned up. "I'll do it."

With one arm wrapped around her narrow waist, he supported her down the staircase to the great room, where he tucked her under a blanket on the sofa. The fireplace logs had burned to embers, so he stacked two in the grate. "Don't move," he ordered before heading into the kitchen.

His mother had always given him a glass of milk and chocolate chip cookies to settle him after a dog fright. The fridge held nothing nonalcoholic to drink except orange juice, so he emptied the carton into a large tumbler. He opened the food pantry doors, saw only cans of soup and the box of cereal he'd purchased on a grocery run, and shrugged. At least the freezer was full of frozen meat, fish, and vegetables. He'd cook her a proper dinner. Then he remembered the bag of oatmeal raisin cookies that Catrina's friend had dropped off earlier that afternoon. He arranged half a dozen on a plate.

"Brigit gave me these cookies. A welcome to Muskoka, she said." He set the juice and cookies on the coffee table.

"Yeah, she wants to welcome you, all right." Catrina frowned. "She stay long?"

"No, I had work to do."

Catrina relaxed into the sofa cushion, tumbler in hand. "Titan," she reminded Chett with one-track-mind firmness that hinted at recovering strength. "The keys to my SUV are in my parka pocket."

"Oh, yeah, I forgot about him," he said, not fooling her for a second. "You want to know my motto? 'It's a dog-eat-dog world, and I'm wearing Milk Bone shorts.' Norm said that in the sitcom *Cheers*." Catrina laughed. Chett didn't.

With mounting unease, he shoved his feet into boots and pulled on his new parka, then gloves for the thick padding—dog bite protection. Chett wasn't taking any chances. He needed his arms and fingers to type.

Outside in the rapidly deepening twilight, key fob in hand, Chett trudged to Catrina's vehicle. French nobility walked faster to the guillotine.

His heart in the vicinity of his tonsils, he unlocked the passenger door, opened it and made the door a shield between him and the beast. Titan, roused out of a snooze, softly woofed a welcome.

That's how they trick you, Chett thought. *They appear docile, even cute when asleep. Awake, they transform into vicious hellhounds. They make little boys pee their pants.*

"Come, Titan," Chett croaked. *Pathetic.* He cleared his thickened throat for an attempt at a manly command. "Come!"

The dog lumbered to its feet on the seat, filling the cab. Its black tail, thick and heavy as a baseball bat, slammed between windshield and headrest. Chett gulped and squeezed his butt cheeks. The massive animal jumped down to the snow-packed drive and jingled the tags on his collar in a hard shake. Then he sniffed the air, not Chett, to his immense, albeit temporary, relief.

No doubt the dog was hungry for his dinner. Hungry enough to sink his teeth into anything that smelled like prey. This police dog's trained nose was especially acute. Spewing fear pheromones like a factory smokestack, Chett slammed the vehicle door and reversed slooowly toward the house, and safety, eyes on the dog in case it lunged.

Titan seemed more interested in doing his business against a tree trunk than in the cowardly excuse for a grown man, but Chett wasn't taking any chances. Then, bladder empty, the beast suddenly streaked like lightning away from the house and across the snow-covered lawn, thunderous barking rolling in his wake.

Chett backed to the stoop, scrabbled behind him for the doorknob, turned it. The door swung wide. He reversed into the house, ducked into the kitchen, and dropped Cat's keys on the island counter. Breathing hard, he pulled gloves off trembling hands. "Catrina, you can call your dog now."

"You call him." She peered over the back of the sofa and spied Chett cowering in the kitchen, boots and all, having left the door wide open. "Oh."

Catrina set her empty glass on the coffee table, wrapped the blanket around her shoulders, and crossed the hardwood floor to the yawning portal that leaked precious heat into the wintery abyss. In case she was still too weak to protect him, Chett remained in the kitchen, the granite-topped island between himself and the open door.

"Titan, come." Cat's authoritative command failed to summon the beast. "He's pretending he didn't hear me." Icy gusts tangled her long curls, and she drew the edges of the blanket close. "Darn rabbits," she grumbled. She put two fingers into her mouth and whistled.

Time stretched like a bungee cord until the jerk, until Titan finally bounded up to his mistress for an ear scratch. Ignoring Chett in the kitchen, the beast ambled across the floor and dropped to the fireplace hearth with a thump that tinkled kitchen cabinet glassware.

Chett released the breath he hadn't realized he was holding. "I need a drink."

Catrina closed the door, crossed to him and patted his shoulder. She intended to comfort, he supposed, yet he felt so…so *emasculated.*

"We'll leave now. The orange juice did the trick. I'm fine."

"Well, I'm not fine, to be honest." He ran an unsteady hand through his hair.

Catrina stilled for a long moment, her gaze locked on his face.

"What?" He flushed, embarrassed by his earlier display of cowardice. Weakness.

"What a pair we make." She unzipped his parka, pulled it down his arms and tossed it on a counter stool.

He lifted his brows. "Are you undressing me?"

She lifted her brows. "It occurred to me that we might put our adrenaline to good use."

"You can't be serious," he protested, even as his member perked in interest.

"From my online research, they say you should counter a bad experience with a good one. Overwrite the memory." She unbuttoned his jeans, slid the zipper down and breached his underwear. His intrigued member filled her palm.

"They make a good point," he said, sliding his hands under the blanket to cup her cooled breasts and nipples that poked through fabric. "So do you."

She arched to increase the pressure, chin upturned, black eyelashes fluttering on snow-white skin. "Still want that drink?"

"Later, Cat." His lips covered hers like they were coming home.

When they surfaced after several minutes of electrifying smooches, she whispered, "I appreciate that you retrieved Titan for me. I understand the courage that took."

Courage? He stored that away to mull over later. In this moment he ached to bury himself inside her. "There are beds upstairs."

"I know." Humor played over kiss-swollen lips. "Titan is happy by the fire."

"Shall we?"

Chett shucked his boots and they climbed the stairs to his bed.

"Don't turn on the light," Cat requested at the door to the master suite he'd taken over. "I don't want to see you. It's pure sex. A mutual physical release. That's all this is."

"A way to chase away the demons."

She exhaled. "You get it."

I get that your demons have it over mine, Kitten. Aloud, he added lightly, "I'm fine with being used for that purpose. Again and again." He closed and locked the door to the hall and tested that it held against a four-legged intruder.

He approached Catrina's dark figure in the dim light, tossed aside the blanket on her shoulders and pulled the cotton turtleneck over her head. He fumbled for a bra clasp and felt only seamless, slippery fabric.

Impatient, she crossed her arms, raised them and pulled off the sports bra. Lush, firm breasts fell into his palms. *Oh, Cat.*

He bent to lick nipple stubs, lip-pull them until she moaned. Last night he'd buried his face between those wonderful breasts.

Before she ran.

Before she declared she never wanted to be with him again.

His breath hitched as he kissed her breasts, her chest, her throat, her lips, that soft, sensitive place behind her ears.

He'd never been on such uncertain ground with a woman. Hey, he'd deserved every label his ex-wife had thrown at him when he crossed the street to avoid people walking dogs: Coward. Childish. Yellow.

He understood rejection based on contempt.

This woman's rejection of him last night was based on fear.

Her fear, not his.

My fear brought her back to me.

Cat's sympathy nudged a tender place he'd been careful to protect from the wicked witch his entire marriage.

But his little head didn't care about all that. His little head wanted to drill to thrill.

His fingers slid down Cat's soft, bare skin, dove under the waistband of her ski pants until they curved around her sweet ass, middle finger sliding, seeking—

Holy Cat! Inside she was wet with want. He lost his train of thought. He quickly ditched his jeans and led her to the bed.

Cat climbed onto the high bed with its antique iron headboard.

For a second he admired her pale nakedness—wanton, willing, waiting—outlined against the patchwork quilt.

A microsecond.

He swallowed. How'd a Hollywood has-been like him get so lucky?

"I'm cold." Arms held out to him—*him!*—Cat invited him to cover her.

He grabbed a condom from the nightstand and complied. Her hand coaxed his swollen member between her legs and into slippery sensation. She tossed her head back and keened with primal, sexual triumph. A mating cry. He almost came right then.

She wrapped her lower limbs around his legs. Ten fingernails stapled his T-shirt to his back. She ground her hips into him fiercely. Deeply. Greedily.

[♬ "Love Me Harder"]

"Harder," she demanded, in the heat of the moment slipping into curling lingo. "Hurry hard."

He angled his pelvis and thrust into paradise. "How's the line?"

"Line's good." She moaned as release swept closer. "Ahhhhh, you're on the button. Burn it. Take me out now." Her back arched. "Now!" she screamed. Her exultant cry echoed off Jenna's vaulted bedroom ceiling.

The beast outside the door erupted in spine-chilling barking, triggering every muscle fiber in Chett's body to contract. Powerful muscular spasms rippled, clenched, until a sensational orgasm rocked him from end to end. Bonelessly he collapsed on Catrina's slick, sated body.

"Good game." She grinned up at him like the Cheshire Cat.

"I gave it my best shot." Chett rolled off her to one side. "Want a rematch?"

"Until you can't move. Bring it on."

CHAPTER 10

The Meat of the Matter

Dammit. I had sex with him again. Twice, to be exact.

Catrina sat on a stool at the kitchen island and watched Chett position three thawed steaks on a tray to slide under the oven broiler. He'd pulled on a pair of sweat pants and a clean white T-shirt after their steamy shower in Jenna's cavernous, decadent bathroom. Catrina coveted a bubble bath in the claw-foot tub under a window overlooking the lake. *Next time.*

She shook her head to banish wishful thinking. *There won't* be *a next time.*

Every hour she spent with him seemed to pry the lid off buried emotions. Today's meltdown had scared the hell out of her. She needed to clamp that lid on tight and walk away. Such a shame, though. He was a fantastic lover.

She dragged her mind out of the bedroom suite. "Why *three* steaks?"

He grinned at her over one broad shoulder. "I don't want Titan to acquire a taste for *raw* meat."

She rolled her eyes and sipped the expensive French pinot noir Chett had chosen to accompany the steaks. Next visit she'd bring a couple bottles to help replenish Jenna's wine cellar. *Dammit.* There wouldn't *be* another rendezvous. Not for dinner, not for costumes, not for making love.

Irked by the internal war setting logic against desire, she snapped, "You're spoiling Titan. Cooked hamburger is good enough."

"Do you think the beast—ah, Titan—understands

bribery? Businesses pay gangs for protection. In this case, steak instead of money."

She laughed, as he no doubt intended. Chett was a master at distracting her from dark thoughts. "I put him in the laundry room. That's your protection."

He moved around the kitchen pulling out plates, cutlery, and napkins. Since she wasn't ever going to be intimate with him again, Catrina decided to satisfy her curiosity and ask the Big Question.

"What happened to give you a fear of dogs?"

She watched his spine stiffen, then deliberately relax. He snagged his glass of wine, seated himself on the counter stool closest to the oven, and hooked his feet on a lower rung. His knee jiggled in unconscious agitation. She placed a calming palm on his thigh.

"I was six, playing catch with some other kids in the park. As I caught the ball, a big dog leaped out of nowhere, knocked me over, and chomped on my right forearm. I can still hear the crunch." A shudder rippled through his lean body. "My visit to Emergency was as terrifying as the bite. The doc reset the bone and sewed up my arm. Seven stitches, followed by a cast and too many painful needles for tetanus, rabies, and whatnot."

She rubbed his thigh. "Titan is highly trained and won't attack unless ordered to."

"My fear has nothing to do with logic." He angled his eyes her way. "If anyone can understand that, it's you."

"Yes," she whispered.

The oven timer dinged. Chett slid off the stool, donned mitts and opened the oven door to remove the steaks.

With his back turned to her, she said, "So it's a good thing that we're not going to...get together again."

The pan clattered onto the gas stove burners. "Who decided that?"

She pulled away from the emotional storm darkening his expression. "I'll be sparing you more trauma."

"Spare me the BS, Cat." He forked steaks onto three plates on the island counter. "My fear is manageable. You can leave Titan at home. You can"—he gestured with his strong chin in the direction of the laundry room off the kitchen—"lock him up."

He allowed her to stew in mutinous silence while he pulled a dish of chopped carrots out of the microwave and spooned them onto two plates.

In a reasonable tone he continued, "I get to decide what I can or cannot handle, not you. Please don't use my fear of dogs as an excuse to cut me loose." He sliced the largest steak into bite-sized chunks, and pushed the plate across the island counter to her with a sheepish grin. "That being said, you may have the honor of feeding your dog."

Cat placed both hands over her stomach. Inside, the ball of resolve to cut Chett loose softened from baseball hard to foam. He had the guts to face *his* fear to be with her. What kind of scaredy-cat did that make her, in comparison? In her entire career she'd never backed down from a challenge. "I need some time."

He shrugged. "So do I. I'm on a deadline. Jenna wants a film concept by Saturday morning. Unfortunately I have to buckle down until I deliver something she likes."

Relief lifted the corners of her mouth. He noticed the involuntary reaction, and dropped a quick kiss on her lips. "I can see how broken up you are, Kitten." He picked up the two plates with carrots and nodded at the plate with chopped steak. "Feed your beast and let's eat."

In five days he'll have forgotten me, she assured herself. *There will not be a next time.* While her psyche rejoiced, a chamber of her heart flooded with unshed tears.

***

Late afternoon the next day, one o'clock L.A. time, Chett speed-dialed Jenna's number. After the preliminaries, he broached the reason for his call. "I have a concept to bounce off you."

"I'm listening."

Splashing in the background distracted him. "Where are you?"

"Reg's pool party." She rattled a drink with ice.

Chett groaned inwardly. Reg Symes, a successful screenwriter and mutual friend, lived in Bel Air. "It's snowing here. Again."

Jenna laughed. "Poor baby." Then she was all business. "What've you got?"

"A female cop with the Drug Enforcement Administration and her drug-sniffing dog track South American drugs smuggled through the Florida Keys."

"No dog, Chett. The audience's focus will be on the animal, not the lead. Hell, the animal companion doesn't even have to be real. Think *Ted* and *Ted 2*."

Chett stared dismally at the content on his laptop that represented twelve hours of his life—characters, theme, goals, motivation, conflict, the three-act structure beats… "You haven't heard the pitch."

"Do I want to be sweating in a uniform in the tropical heat for a couple of months while filming? No, I do not."

He had to ask. "Has Reg got anything for you?"

"Two of his action screenplays are optioned by big studios. Another is in development with an indie production company." She noisily slurped her cold drink.

Rub it in, why don't you, Chett groused. Outside, a pickup with an attached blade plowed the lane clear of a foot of fresh snow. "You were saying about the indie company property?"

"Sorry, a studio exec just walked by." She lowered the

decibel level to relay, "The producers are waiting on an expression of interest from Marianna Martinez before they cast the female lead."

Marianna, a twenty-something actor with a killer figure, had won the Golden Globe award that Jenna coveted. "That's too bad," Chett commiserated.

"Yeah," Jenna replied with feeling. After a long pause that spoke to the depths of her frustration, she admitted, "I'm having lunch with Trudy Malcovitch tomorrow. She's the casting director for *Apollo: Intergalactic War*."

"*Variety.com* reported that they'd already cast the female lead."

"The superhero apparently has a mother on his home planet."

Chett heard the catch in her voice, and wished he could give her a hug. "I'll have something for you by Saturday morning. I promise."

"I'm counting on you, darling." She signed off.

Crestfallen by her rejection of his drug-sniffing dog handler concept, Chett told himself to focus on the positive—Jenna hadn't yet found a suitable screenplay. He had a chance to redeem himself. On the other hand, he'd been holed up in Muskoka for a week with nothing to show for it.

Three days remained to craft a pitch that'd reboot an aging sex goddess's career as well as his own. Chett released a dispirited sigh, closed the document on the laptop screen, and dragged it to the trash can icon.

All out of ideas and fresh food, he decided to drive into town to eat.

***

Bob, the muscular, tattooed Tim Hortons assistant manager in his early twenties, took Chett's order for coffee and a sandwich. "How's your screenplay coming?"

Chett plastered on a winning smile that belied the fact his career had cratered. "It's coming." He tapped his temple. "Getting the scenes out of my head and onto the page takes time."

"Gotcha." Sympathy quenched Bob's fan-flushed excitement. Apparently the guy wasn't easily fooled by BS. He tipped his round head at a dark bulk sitting alone at a table by the window. "Do you know Henrik Muller? He works for Richard Cairncross, the producer."

"I've met Dick Cairncross." The famous producer had more than a dozen international hits to his credit. They'd met briefly at a party a decade ago.

"*Shooting the Enemy*, starring Vin Diesel. *Midnight Detail* starring Matt Damon."

"You know your action movies." Chett picked up his Double-double coffee and handed Bob a purple Canadian ten-dollar bill.

"Ya got that right." Bob's pleasant round face beamed. "Grab a table and I'll bring your sandwich over when it's ready. Here's your change."

"Keep it."

Chett walked over to Henrik Muller who was flipping through his smartphone. He extended a hand. "Henrik? I'm Chett de Groot, a screenwriter."

The broad-shouldered stranger with mountain-range biceps and pecs straining the fabric of his black turtleneck raised his massive dark head. Chett checked his movie memory for an actor with a busted nose and rapier-thin white scar slashing the left cheek from eye to chin. Henrik owned a face that would make a mugger think twice.

Henrik waved at the chair opposite. "Have a seat. Do I know your work?" The words rumbled out like Arnold Schwarzenegger's dialogue in the *Terminator* film franchise—clipped, no-nonsense, accented.

"*Mafia Massacre.*" When that didn't get a sign of recognition, Chett added, "*Undercover Slasher.*"

The big man nodded. "Call me Henry. You won't have heard of me. Nonspeaking parts, mostly. A gladiator in a Ridley Scott movie. Aliens in several sci-fi films. A warrior in several *Game of Thrones* battle scenes." He sipped his coffee. "I've been killed off a dozen times in that series."

Chett chuckled. At that moment Bob delivered a small tray with Chett's turkey sandwich. "Bob here says you work for Dick Cairncross."

Henry's nod simultaneously confirmed the statement and acknowledged the younger man. "Part-time, depending on my schedule. Up here at Dick's Canadian lake house, I'm his majordomo—a combo of security chief and butler. His L.A. staff refuses to cross the border."

Or can't, Chett speculated. He took a bite of his sandwich, stalling for time until Bob took the hint and reluctantly returned to his position behind the counter.

A twinkle lit Henry's somber dark eyes. "You have a script to pitch to Cairncross." He stated this without rancor.

Chett set his sandwich aside. "The fact of the matter is, I have no script." He explained that Jenna had commissioned a spec action screenplay with a suitable lead role for her, and he was out of ideas. He got straight to the point. "What might interest your boss?"

Henry guffawed. "That's easy. Fast women, fast boats. He has a summer place on this big lake because it gives him the privacy to indulge in both."

"Boats?"

"Powerboats with serious engines," he clarified. "Some days Lake Muskoka is as smooth as glass. Going flat out you almost fly over the water. On a lake there are no ocean swells to slow you down. His current boat can reach 150 mph, and he has a new twin-engine model on order. He's shooting for 200 mph."

"He sounds like a risk taker."

Henry lifted one boulder of a shoulder. "It's managed risk. Cairncross is a smart man. Sure, he took a few calculated risks, had to, in order to make it in this business."

Chett was thoughtful. "Powerboats, huh?"

"He also collects vintage boats. He enjoys showing them off at Muskoka antique and classic boat events each summer." Henry finished his coffee, pushed the cup aside, and directed a level gaze at Chett. "I can assure you that he'd read an action script with high-speed boat chases. *Undercover Slasher* gives you cred." He pushed back his chair, stood Hulk tall, and pulled out his wallet. "Here's my card. Call me when you've written a treatment, and I'll put it in front of him."

"Hey, thanks, man." Chett retrieved one of his own cards and handed it over. "I'll return the favor someday."

Henry winked. "I expect nothing less." He pulled a worn leather biker jacket off the back of his chair. "Good luck."

After Henry left, Chett sat connecting the *B*s while his coffee cooled, forgotten. *Boats. Bahamas. Bad guys. Babe in bikini.*

[♫ "Speedboat Chase"]

CHAPTER 11

Skating on Thin Ice

Chett holed up in the lake house and wrote straight through the rest of the week. Saturday at midday he attached the high concept and treatment for an action film tentatively titled *Kingpin of the Sea* to an email and pressed the send button.

Sure, it was derivative. A foreign crime boss smuggles drugs into the Florida Keys via powerboats. When an undercover agent with the Drug Enforcement Agency infiltrates his organization and becomes the drug lord's mistress, the danger escalates. Several high-speed ocean chases and blown-up boats later, the good guys win.

To please Jenna, he'd ensured she'd be out of uniform and wearing risqué costumes for most of the movie. He'd even written in a yacht with a sunbathing deck on which to display the figure she so desperately wanted to show off.

On her end, Jenna had arranged for Dick Cairncross to be invited to the Malibu party that evening. Jenna, her manager, and her agent had the entire day to read the document and rehearse the pitch. He'd done his part. Now it was up to them to work their contacts to generate interest in the project.

Chett laced numb fingers together and stretched his arms in front of him. He glanced at the half-full bottle of whisky on the sideboard and realized he hadn't swallowed so much as a dram in days—unprecedented since his divorce. As he closed the laptop, he felt an unfamiliar emotion—satisfaction with his creative effort. He figured he deserved a break from the keyboard.

Outside, snow crystals sparkled in sunlight. Water dripped from thick icicles hanging from the eaves. The outdoor temperature had risen to bearable. He decided to check out the local winter carnival.

***

Chett found a parking space among the cars, SUVs, and pickups lining the streets in downtown Port Carson, and dropped his keys into his parka pocket. Down a slope and along the shoreline, people of all ages sat at picnic tables or under canvas tents that kept out the cool breeze. Service club volunteers at smoking BBQs offered burgers and hot dogs for two bucks each. Chett bought a burger and a steaming hot chocolate to wash it down, then surveyed the scene.

Four snowmobiles roared along a track the length of two football fields on the lake parallel to the shore. Farther out on the snow-covered ice, snowbanks defined the perimeter of a rectangular ice rink. Helmeted players in a mismatched collection of hockey jerseys slapped a puck back and forth.

Chett sauntered toward the dozens of spectators clustered around the ice rink. Children perched on adult shoulders, the better to see the action. According to Bob, the Tim Hortons gossip maven, Goldie Hawn had owned a Muskoka summer home for years, and her son was up visiting friends. He wondered whether Wyatt, an actor and goalie, had joined the game.

Chett scanned the crowd, stopping at three men standing side by side, all comedy royalty from movie classics such as *American Pie*, *Three Amigos*, and *Austin Powers*. The woman at his shoulder, insulated coffee mug in hand, noticed his interest.

"That guy in the blue toque is Eugene Levy, up here stayin' with Martin Short. Beside them is Mike Myers in the red and black plaid jacket. They're putting on a benefit tonight for autistic children at the Sterling Inn."

Those three improv artists together on stage promised a riot of laughs. Chett wondered if Catrina planned to attend. "Are tickets available?"

She snickered. "Yeah, at a thousand bucks a pop. They're counting on their rich friends to come through." Observing his disappointment, she patted his arm. "I hear an HBO crew is in town to film the show."

A shriek cut through the cries of encouragement from hockey fans. As one, the crowd turned to the right of the rink where a long strip of yellow caution tape marked the perimeter of the winter carnival area on the lake ice. Well beyond the tape, a small girl in a pink snowsuit was making a beeline toward a red balloon bobbing in the breeze.

"Oh my gawd," the woman beside him breathed. "Lilly is heading straight for trouble. An underground stream bubbles out and weakens the ice there. She's only three. She's doesn't know any better." Her voice rose on a note of hysteria. "What's her mother thinking, to let Lilly wander like that?" She whipped out her cell phone and punched in 911.

Out of nowhere, an enormous black dog leaped over the yellow tape and streaked toward the little girl. Chett's heart lurched. Bile rose as he involuntarily recalled the excruciating pain of a dog's jaws clamped on his own arm. He had to save her from the same fate. Or worse.

Heart pumping, Chett leaped over the tape and ran, ran as if his own life depended on reaching the girl before that monster.

Someone slammed into him from the left, flattened him face down in slushy snow. A knee across his back, his right arm twisted behind him, and he was immobilized before he had a chance to spit the slush out of his mouth.

"What the *hell* are you doing?" a familiar voice hissed in his ear.

Catrina! He had to warn her of the danger but she'd knocked the breath out of him. Struggling mightily for enough breath to speak, he finally croaked, "That dog is after the little girl."

"That dog is Titan, and he's working. If I let you up do you promise to stay put?"

What choice do I have? He agreed. The knee lifted. Seriously worried she'd crushed his spine, he tentatively pushed himself to a kneeling position. The cold slush soaked through his jeans, and his entire body shuddered. Stuntmen made recovery from a take down look easy. Chett felt like he'd been crushed by a tank.

"Stay there," Catrina commanded. Abandoning him, she raised her arms high, raised her voice even higher to be heard above the cacophony of voices shouting at the child. "Remain behind the tape. Titan is a trained police dog. He's retrieving the girl. Safety first, people. Stay calm. Let the police dog do his job." She repeated the message until the crowd quieted to wait and watch.

Each draw of the crisp fresh air burned Chett's bronchial tubes. He wiped melted snow from his eyes with a shaking gloved hand. He'd been literally flattened by a real-life manifestation of his action movie heroines. When his vision cleared, he watched Titan use his nose and the side of his body to gently nudge the little girl and herd her toward Catrina and safety.

"Baby, my baby." The anguished screams of a woman in a matching pink parka broke the silence. A hundred and fifty feet out on the ice, still in the danger zone, the child halted and refused to move, frightened to tears.

Catrina sprinted over to a man struggling to restrain the frantic woman from bursting through the yellow tape. "Madam, be quiet," Chett heard Catrina order in a no-nonsense cop tone. "You're scaring her. Plus"—Catrina added loud enough for the bystanders to hear—"I don't want to have to rescue you too." The woman, crazed with desperation, ignored Cat.

She waved over a couple of hockey players. "Grab an arm and hold on to this woman. The ice is too thin out there to support an adult's weight."

The mother surged and bucked to free herself from the men's tight hold on her upper arms. "Let go of me. My baby's out there. Heeeellllp," she screeched at the top of her lungs. Her frenzied cries raised the hair on the back of Chett's neck.

"Scarf," Catrina barked like a surgeon ordering a scalpel. When one appeared, she wrapped it across the woman's mouth and tied it to muzzle her.

Chett stood on wobbly legs and staggered over to offer help. He observed pure hatred in the mother's eyes. If anything happened to her daughter, Catrina was a dead woman, for sure. In the ensuing silence he felt the breeze strengthen. Grey clouds scuttled across the sun. He shivered, chilled to the bone.

"What's the kid's name?" Catrina asked the scarf donor, a teenage girl.

"Lilly. I'm her babysitter." Tears rolled down her cheeks. "I'm so scared."

"Don't be. Lilly is upset but doing fine. See?" The little girl had wrapped her arms around Titan's neck and buried her face in his fur. Catrina addressed the agitated crowd. "Quiet, please, all of you. Give us some space."

Muttering, the crowd responded to her authority and backed off from the tape, leaving a clear line of vision between the tiny girl and her mother. Only a few minutes had passed—insufficient time for emergency responders to arrive.

"Lilly, come to your mother," Catrina enunciated slowly in a clear, calm voice. "She wants you."

A plaintive wail whispered across the expanse of ice on a frigid current of air. "Is she mad at me?"

"No, honey, no, she's not mad. She just wants you and the dog. Bring Titan with you, okay? Titan, find child." The big dog responded to her command by nudging the girl in their direction.

"Good girl, Lilly," Cat praised as the tiny girl took two tentative steps. "I have treats for you and Titan."

"What kind of treats?" she yelled back, dubious about the bribe, patently worried she was in trouble.

Catrina dug into her parka pocket, pulled out a box of candy and waved it. "I've got Smarties."

"I want another balloon," Lilly shouted stubbornly, "if I can't have that one." The tyke swiveled and took a couple of steps in the direction of the far-off red balloon until Titan blocked her. The hockey players barely maintained their hold on the freaked-out woman who'd apparently developed supermom strength. The anxious crowd surged against the tape, calling to her, Catrina's request for quiet forgotten.

"We'll get you another balloon. Two balloons." Cat's strong voice carried over the others. "Better balloons," she promised, beckoning to the babysitter. "Get me a couple of red balloons."

Moments later, two gas-filled red balloons duly collected from parents clutching their children, Catrina wound a forefinger around the strings and waggled it in the air. Out on the dangerously thin ice, Lilly decided the balloons to be a worthy bribe. She lifted short legs to clomp though snowdrifts, Titan's nose at her backside.

Anxious seconds crept by. When Lilly was finally within ten feet of the yellow tape, Catrina walked out to meet her. She hoisted the child into her arms, and the crowd vented its relief in cheers.

"Come, Titan," Catrina commanded, and the threesome closed the distance to the woman and her captors. With a sob, she snatched the child from Catrina.

Lilly withstood her mother's hug and kisses for a few seconds, then erupted in a fresh wail. "I want my balloons!"

Catrina handed them off and slipped through the crowd encircling mother and daughter. She crouched to stroke Titan's back, rub the soft fur under his ears and feed him a dog biscuit. "Good dog, what a smart dog," she crooned. "You're a hero." She snapped a leash onto his harness.

Admiration for Catrina's quick action washed over Chett. She was powerful. In control. Confident and decisive. Superbly competent. He approached her from the right, away from Titan. Even hero dogs bit.

He slapped Catrina heartily on the back. "Since none of these ungrateful locals seems to want to congratulate you, I will. Good work, Officer." He grinned at her discomfited glare. "You're trained to deal with situations." He tagged the milling crowd. "The rest of us hadn't a clue how to react. Being a cop is who you are."

"I did what I had to, what anyone would." Her clipped statement demanded an end to the discussion.

Chett demurred. "Then why didn't they?" When she had no answer, he continued, "You and Titan are heroes. I, on the other hand, allowed my childhood trauma to override good sense in an emergency situation."

He noticed she didn't argue. Instead she said, "The extra training I gave Titan to track lost children paid off today."

He noticed the jiggle along the leash held by one gloved hand. He gripped her elbow, anxious to steer her to someplace warm, out of the deepening cold that stung exposed skin. The nearby Muskoka Laker Brew Pub adjacent to the town park fit the bill. "Can I be the first to buy you a drink?"

"Later," she said. "I have things to do. A report to make." She inclined her head at two male cops striding across boot-packed snow in their direction. On shore, lights flashed on the roof of an Ontario Provincial Police patrol car. "The OPP took their time getting here from Bracebridge," she snapped.

"There's no cop stationed in Port Carson? Today demonstrates there's a case to be made for one," Chett opined loud enough to be overheard, generating interested glances in his direction. "I'll leave you to deal with your colleagues."

She rolled her eyes. "Keep your voice down. They're not colleagues."

"Yet." He ceded the ground, or rather lake, to the new arrivals. Callouts had to be documented. She'd be occupied for a while with the report.

Curiously deflated, Chett headed for his vehicle, alone and lonely for the woman who personified the beautiful kickass female cops he'd written into his action screenplays. Cat acted in an emergency like she was born to it, with her and Titan operating as a stellar unit to diffuse the crisis.

I discovered my fantasy woman in the Great White North, but sooner or later I have to return to Hollywood.

A titan-sized lump in his throat predicted it wasn't going to be easy.

CHAPTER 12

That's Amore

Catrina's doorbell rang at six that evening. On her small porch, Chett stamped fresh snow off his western leather boots. He balanced a pizza box on one palm and gripped a liquor store paper bag with the other hand. A plastic grocery bag dangled from a forearm. Behind him, town streetlights pricked the black night like a string of holiday lights.

She squinted. A thick black line curved above his upper lip. "What on earth is that on your face? Black felt marker?"

His grin straightened the fake mustache and punched dimples into wind-reddened cheeks. "Are you going to invite me in? This pizza is flash freezing as we speak."

She hesitated. The days apart had given her plenty of time to think. To miss him. To get over him. To crush the desire to be intimate with him again. Being with him stimulated emotions. She'd spent years *stifling* emotions.

However...

She was starving. In all the drama that afternoon at the carnival and its aftermath, she'd forgotten to buy groceries. The pizza smelled delicious. So did the scent of musky aftershave wafting on the Arctic draft. Determination to avoid him melted like a snowball in a frying pan.

Rescuing the child that afternoon had boosted her confidence. She'd handled a crazed mother determined to run headlong onto dangerously thin ice. *Surely I can handle a Hollywood writer. I'll send him home after dinner.*

Scratch that.

I'll send him home after dinner and a quickie.

She capitulated to temptation and stepped back. "I am hungry," she admitted.

His Hollywood-white teeth flashed and he waggled his brows. He knew she knew that *she* wasn't talking about food.

In her foyer, Chett toed off his boots and tossed his parka over the back of a white wicker chair. Mustached, with gelled blond hair, and wearing a black long-sleeved shirt and thin white tie, he looked hot as all hell.

[♬ "That's Amore"]

She swallowed. A primal hunger surged in her nether region. Of its own volition her gaze dropped to the crotch bulge in his tight black jeans. "Who are you supposed to be?"

"Vito Corleone, at your service." He bowed.

The name rang a distant bell. "A mob boss?" she hazarded.

He smirked. "*The Godfather* is one of my all-time favorite films—a classic." He pointed at the plastic grocery bag hanging from her fingers. "I brought a reward for Titan."

At the mention of his name, the German shepherd's black ears angled to attention. He lifted his long black nose from his paws for an interested sniff. Catrina thumbed open the bag to peer inside. "Another cooked steak?"

He shrugged. "The bribe worked last time."

"It's a smart way to make friends. Next you'll be patting him," she teased.

He paled under his California tan. "Maybe another time," he croaked. He pulled a bottle of red wine from the paper bag. "I have something for you, too. Italian."

"Of course. What else would Vito drink?" She placed the pizza box on the old leather-strapped steamer trunk that served as a coffee table and headed for the compact kitchen.

"Titan has already eaten his dinner. I'll save the steak until tomorrow. Have a seat," she invited over her shoulder while she wrapped the steak to store in the fridge.

Anticipation bubbled below her calm surface. He amused her, he turned her on. She placed a couple of wine glasses, plates, cutlery, and serviettes on a white wood tray and carried it to the antique trunk, a relic from the days when steamboats conveyed tourists to Lake Muskoka resorts.

Chett perched straight-backed at one end of her navy slipcovered sofa, a position with a direct sightline to Titan. Keeping one eye on the lounging dog, Chett twisted off the wine bottle cap and poured.

He handed her a glass and raised his. Solemnly he toasted, "To your and Titan's heroism today." He sipped, his baby blues above the glass filled with undeniable respect.

"Don't you start in on my *calling* as a police officer," she warned. Sure, rescuing the child with Titan's help had made her feel good. But that rescue was a one-time thing. Period. "The cops eventually arrived. If I hadn't taken action, the little girl would have been just fine."

"Did they have a trained dog? How would they have rescued the kid?" he asked, raising a questioning brow.

"Safety lines and drysuits," she mumbled.

"Those two cops marched on the scene dressed for patrol. I didn't see any safety lines or drysuits."

"No." Even she had to admit that much. "I'm sure they called the rescue team."

"More delay. You and Titan averted what could very well have been a tragedy." Chett transferred a slice of pizza loaded with cheese, bacon, pepperoni, and sliced vegetables to his plate. "Actions illuminate character. I learned that in film school. You stepped up and took action. That makes you a hero."

She didn't have a comeback, so she devoured two delicious pizza slices, the better to bury uncomfortable feelings churning her stomach. He'd return to California soon. Surely he'd made progress on a screenplay. He hadn't left Jenna's lake house in days or Catrina would have heard about it. No one in Port Carson kept secrets for long.

Except me.

Well, Chett knew her secret, but after he returned to L.A. her private struggle with PTSD would be safe again. Full, she leaned back against the cushions. "How's the script coming along?"

Chett pushed away his empty plate and refilled their wine glasses. "According to studio scuttlebutt, they're looking for another *True Lies* or James Bond-type story involving international intrigue. Mickey McNichol, my agent, tells me the studios want sophisticated scripts for action films that they can easily dub into various languages and sell overseas. There's a lot of money in foreign sales. Everybody, including me, wants to make a pile of money."

He sighed, leaned back against the cushions, and propped his feet on the trunk, as comfortable in her space as if he lived there. "An action script is certainly doable on my end, but Jenna insists that it be a vehicle for her comeback. Her demands are killing me. She wants a meaty starring role that showcases her acting skills, but nevertheless she refuses to dump the pinup girl persona. She wants to be a babe—an ageing babe, mind you—who's taken seriously as an actor." He drained his glass. "She can't have it both ways," he added with conviction.

Catrina waved a languid hand. The wine and food had worked magic, relaxing her after the stressful afternoon. "The beautiful and talented Halle Berry, Scarlett Johansson, and Kim Basinger were all nominated for acting awards. Halle Berry won—"

"All right, already." He tilted his empty wine glass at her in tribute. "I grant you the point. I guess what I'm really saying is that writing a female lead character is out of my comfort zone."

"You mean a female character with a brain?" She had him like a perp pinned to the floor, and smirked at his discomfort. Back to her real question. "How far along is the script?"

He leaned to set his wine glass on the tray. "The script for tonight?" he replied, dodging her query. "Sorry, there's nothing on paper. However, I did create a scenario involving a mob boss and a female cop that may interest you."

"Si." She set her glass beside his.

"See what?"

She laughed. "*Si* as in yes, it interests me. We *are* Italian in this scenario?"

"Not you." He swiveled to face her. "You're from a big Irish family and grew up in Brooklyn. In high school you had a crush on an extremely handsome, intelligent, charming, witty—"

"I get the drift," Catrina interrupted wryly.

"Italian-American boy," he continued. "Your cop father forbid a relationship because the boy's family was connected with the Mafia."

"Very *Romeo and Juliet*."

He ignored her comment. "Then you followed in your father's footsteps and became a cop."

"You're not far wrong, there. And my grandmother was Irish," she murmured.

"After the young man's father ended up wearing cement shoes at the bottom of the Hudson River, the son took over the shady family business. He now runs an East Coast theft ring, stealing cars and shipping them overseas. The rookie female cop goes undercover to investigate him and his pals and gather evidence. Bullets and sparks fly."

"Why doesn't he recognize the cop from high school?"

He shrugged. "It was a big school. He was a senior and she a freshman. He never noticed her."

She laughed. "You have an answer for everything. How about this? Tell me you didn't merely 'borrow'—she pantomimed air quotes—the *Mafia Massacre* concept for tonight's scenario. I told you I hate watching those movies."

He nodded. "I heard you. Believe me, I don't want my screenplays to alienate the female half of the audience, including you. Listen for a minute. Every action film sets a protagonist who is the power for good against an antagonist who represents the wrong side of the law. That's the conflict. Then we ramp up the conflict with expressions of power—weapons, explosions, fight scenes, car chases, or whatever. Extreme action gets the audience's blood pumping and furthers the conflict. Viewers are happy when good trumps evil and the guy gets the girl."

She raised her brows. "Or the girl gets the guy."

He raised a forefinger. "Point taken. The success of *Wonder Woman* did teach the industry that a female protagonist can carry a blockbuster movie." He placed one warm hand on her knee—a physical connection to bolster his next words. In a husky voice that stirred the sensual pot, he said, "On the way over here I thought about what might happen if the good girl and the bad guy are conflicted by the power of mutual sexual attraction. The power of passion. Who wins then?"

Catrina considered. "If the good girl wins and puts him away, she loses the guy. Double conflict. At least it puts the relationship front and center. Is this from the screenplay you're writing?"

He lifted a shoulder. "Possibly. I'm still working it out in my head." Then twisted his lips into an exaggerated lecherous smile. "You do inspire me." He swung her upper body across his knees, tipped her back in his arms, and lowered his mouth to whisper, "On many levels."

The pressure of his firm lips on hers sent a shiver to the tips of her toes. Their tongues tangled, slippery and warm and spicy. Heat from the gas fireplace warmed her skin. Deep kisses heated her blood. His lips left hers bereft as he kissed her eyelids, the sensitive skin at her temples, the tip of her nose, her throat, as he stoked the furnace that was her core.

"So I'm powerful?" she asked, sliding her lips along his freshly shaved jawline. She inhaled musk and wood smoke and fresh air, the divine scent almost as erotically charged as the large palm curved over one breast, thumb sweeping the nipple.

He laved her earlobe with his thick agile tongue. The tingling sensation released her tight neck muscles, and her head dropped into the curve of his shoulder. Dreamily she thought that this sweet expertise implied significant practice with other women. But she wasn't arguing.

"You are very powerful," he replied at last. "I've only just realized how much power you have."

Was this part of the scenario? "Explain."

"You have power over Titan. Power over others. Power over me."

At the moment she did not feel terribly powerful. On the contrary, *his* seductive power had her in a needy haze of desire. She needed to redress the balance. "I do have an appropriate prop," she mused.

He lifted his head to look into her eyes. She'd caught his attention.

"Handcuffs."

CHAPTER 13

Power is the great aphrodisiac.
– Henry A. Kissinger

Scant minutes later, Chett lay spread-eagled and gloriously naked on the bed, both wrists handcuffed to the painted antique iron spindle headboard. Catrina had banished Titan to a blanket on the kitchen floor on the other side of the locked bedroom door, rather than sleep in his customary spot on the bedside mat. She wanted Chett calm. Relaxed. Focused on her and nothing else.

The soulful voices of Laura Pausini and Andrea Bocelli, suave Italian tenor, surged through the small speakers attached to Catrina's smartphone on the nightstand.

[♬ "Dare to Live"]

Crouched on the mattress at his hip, she trailed a finger along the centerline dip in his abs, down to his groin. No tan line. "Do you sunbathe nude?" The finger curved up the length of his baton-stiff member.

Chett inhaled, then blew out on a breath the demand, "Take off your clothes."

"We wouldn't want the fun to be over too quickly, now would we?" She licked her finger and circled the sensitive tip.

Through gritted teeth, he warned, "If you keep this up, I can't control the outcome."

She snickered at the wordplay. "I'll take it slow."

He twigged to her slit-eyed, devious intent and flung his head onto the pillow. "You plan to torture me."

"I'm merely interested in seeing how long you can last before—"

"Blastoff?"

"Precisely." It would not do to stimulate him beyond the point of no return. Yet. Time for a diversion. "Women's nipples are incredibly sensitive. Are yours?" Her lips encased one tiny bud, then the other.

"I think it depends on the man," he gasped. "And wonder of wonders, I'm one of them. I never knew—I never felt—" He arched his neck and gave himself over to the sensations.

"You're more sensitive than I gave you credit for." She tongue-flicked the closest nipple until it peaked.

"How so?"

"I assumed you were one of those *all action, all the time* guys."

"Like your co-workers?"

That dart struck home. "*Former* co-workers. You are *nothing* like my former Marine Unit colleagues. Cops live to save the world. In contrast, you entertain the world." She gently nipped a nipple.

"Ouch. That's what writers do. Our job is to enable viewers to escape their lives for a couple of hours."

"Real life sucks sometimes," she agreed. Her mouth descended to encase the end of his wilting shaft. Her tongue massaged the sensitive tip until the length swelled and stretched and stiffened. She withdrew, satisfied with her efforts. "When did you last commit your heart and mind to *your* job?"

He squirmed. His entrapped wrists rattled the duo of handcuffs attached to either end of her headboard. "Why the interrogation?"

"Because I can. You don't have a monopoly on the hard questions."

"And if I refuse to answer?" he lashed out, defiant.

She laughed softly, and rubbed her finger over the moist end of the shaft standing at attention. "I start. Stop. Resume. Stop. I don't mind if this takes all night."

He groaned. "You're killing me."

She fisted his member and circled the end with her tongue before inquiring smoothly, "Who or what made you sell out?"

He lurched, and the metal handcuffs rattled the headboard. "Low blow."

She pursed her mouth and blew a stream of air on his oh-so-sensitive tip until he moaned. "I'm waiting for an answer."

"I wanted to sell my screenplays."

"And?"

"I wanted the trappings of success—beautiful wife, imported car, money. And I got it. All of it."

"And then?"

Stormy eyes glared. "I lost all of it. Satisfied?"

She kissed the thin line of his lips until they softened, let her in. "And now?"

"Now I'm having fun for the first time in a decade. Excluding tonight," he qualified. "Tonight you're driving me crazy."

"Join the club."

His body and his eyes stilled, mirroring Titan on alert. "You're not crazy. PTSD isn't crazy."

She sat up, not liking where this was going. "You don't know anything about PTSD."

Sympathy smoothed the lines around his mouth. "Tell me."

"Not tonight." *Never.*

She drew upright, pulled her shirt over her head, popped the clasp on her new lace demi-cup bra, and gave him an eyeful designed to forestall more probing of the verbal variety. She was all for probing of the physical variety. She needed him to fill her with exquisite pleasure, to drive out the demons, at least for a few hours.

Her full breasts pressed against his firm chest as she kissed her way along his jaw and behind his ear. Her busy lower hand cupped his balls and stroked the soft skin. "Are you ready to do my bidding?"

"What do you want from me?" he hissed between clenched teeth, fighting for control.

She thought about that. What she really wanted, she couldn't have—him in her bed every night for the rest of the long, cold winter. "I want to read the screenplay."

"Not ready," he managed, breathing ragged. "All I've finished so far is the treatment. Sent it to Jenna this morning."

"That's progress," she agreed. "You deserve a reward." She slid off the bed and stepped out of jeans and lace panties. She noted with relief that his features broadcast ravenous lust, the issue of her PTSD swept aside.

"Condoms are in my pants."

His gaze followed her breasts as she stooped to retrieve his jeans on the floor. She pulled a strip from a back pocket and held it up. "Six?"

"I can't get enough of you. I want you *now*."

"You forget who's in charge," she purred as she unrolled the condom. Then she straddled him and dangled her breasts over his face. "Take me in your mouth."

As his agile lips closed over one nipple, sensation spiraled down her spine to pool like molten lava in her groin. She arched her back, gave him access to the other nipple. With one hand she rubbed the soft tip of his member against her moist lower lips. His hips twisted as he attempted to thrust the engorged shaft inside.

"So needy," she whispered, rubbing the hard length of

him against the hypersensitive skin folds. "We're on my timetable, not yours."

At that he sucked on the skin of her left breast, hard.

"No hickeys." She sat up out of his reach and laughed. "Play nice, and I'll give you what you want. What we both want."

"I want you," he said forcefully, heated glance flashing from her face to her breasts. "I've wanted nothing but you since that night you wore the lizard costume. I can't concentrate. I can't think of anything but you."

"You sound like you're in love." She said it lightly, but her heart fractured because she knew it couldn't possibly be true and, heaven help her, she wanted it to be true.

"I want to make love to you more than anything in this world."

It was enough. Because she wanted his hands steadying her wild hips, she reached to release his wrists from the handcuffs and tossed them aside.

Straddling him, she slid his slick, hard-to-bursting member deep inside. Both sighed.

Starting slow, building momentum, she rode him as he thrust and gyrated his pelvis like a mechanical bull. They drove each other higher, faster, until her vision, her mind, everything blanked except the burst of ecstasy. Her inner muscles clenched him, bonded them in a mutual explosive orgasm.

The wall protecting her heart shattered. Strong emotion gushed, filling her body like helium until she floated in a natural high.

Is this what love feels like?

Sated, exhausted, cheeks damp with tears, she tumbled off Chett, curled against his warmth and fell off a cliff into oblivion.

Until the nightmare.

CHAPTER 14

Nothing makes us so lonely as our secrets. – Paul Tournier

A primal scream shocked Chett out of a dream in which Big Joe had backed his bride, Prudence, against a tree outside in deep snow, lifted her heavy woolen skirts, and was shoving his dick into warm, wet heaven.

He opened his eyes to find himself blind in the pitch-dark bedroom. The scream faded under the weight of wall-shaking barking that flattened him to the mattress. His heart slammed into his ribs like a battering ram.

Oh, wait. That was a hundred pounds of dog slamming against the flimsy bedroom door. Chett scooted backwards until his head hit the headboard. The only other exit, a window, was located beside the doorway to hell. He was trapped!

"No, not the girls!"

Catrina's anguished cry soared above Titan's frenzied barking, a feat of lung power he attributed to her years of yelling orders at criminals.

"What girls? Where?" Confusion pierced Chett's great fear of becoming the beast's midnight snack.

For an answer, a fist whizzed by his knee and landed a solid punch on the mattress.

He rolled out of bed, out of range, and turned on the bedside lamp. Catrina's limbs thrashed, her eyes were open but unseeing, her features were crimped with horror. In that moment Chett realized she was immersed in a nightmare, lost to the real world, to any conscious awareness of her actions, to the beat of pounding thumps against the door, to him.

Chett reined in an overwhelming impulse to hide in the closet or under the bed, safe from the threat of being eaten alive by a berserk dog. A panic attack would *not* serve either of them. Logic implied there was method to the dog's madness. Titan wasn't targeting him. He wanted to reach Catrina.

The certainty of that fact did not slow Chett's racing pulse. He ran around to Catrina's side of the bed and vigorously shook her bare shoulder. "Wake up, Cat. You're here with me. Safe."

All he got for his humanitarian effort was a powerful two-handed shove that sent him stumbling back until he hit the wall. *Holy Cat, she's strong.* Luckily only his ego was bruised. Apparently the normal route wasn't the way to bring her out of the hell she was reliving.

Catrina writhed on the bed, continuing to battle unseen monsters. He recalled that, after falling asleep in his arms at Jenna's place, Cat had woken up agitated and insisted on going home to her dog. He didn't understand then, but his poor excuse for a brain finally got the message. Right now Catrina needed her dog more than she needed Chett.

Titan again slammed his full body weight against the door. Wood splintered. The next charge, and he'd be through. Chett, muscles geared for flight, scanned the room. *Options. What are my options?*

Think, damn it! The canine jaws of steel that clamped on escaping criminals could also nudge a little girl to safety. He'd witnessed it with his own eyes. Catrina was *not* in danger from Titan. Her demons resided in haunting memories.

Chett gulped and made the only decision any terrified human would do. He opened the door and hid behind it. Titan shot through the opening faster than a speeding bullet and skidded to a halt at Cat's shoulder.

The dog's deafening barks ricocheted off walls, the ceiling, the hardwood floor. Chett clamped his palms to his ears and kept an eye on it. Titan's massive snout nudged Catrina's shoulder. Calming in the presence of his mistress, Titan's barks slowed, lowered in volume, became insistent as if following a well-practiced script.

Finally Catrina extended a trembling arm and wrapped it around Titan's head. "Good boy. Good boy," she soothed in a raspy, raw voice that sawed Chett's rusty heartstrings.

"Catrina, are you okay?" he called from the doorway.

She levered herself up on elbows to locate him. "What're you doing way over there? Aren't you cold?"

Goosebumps pebbled his bare skin. He realized he was freezing. "Don't change the subject."

He took a step to be with her, comfort her, but the formidable guard dog's evil eyes and warning woof persuaded him to rethink that plan. He cupped his dangling member protectively. "Tell Titan it wasn't my fault."

Catrina swung her legs over the edge of the bed and reached for a robe hanging from a hook. "He'll relax when I give him a treat." She shook her head. "Better yet, you do it. Meet me in the kitchen."

She waited while Chett hurried to his side of the bed, and left the room with the dog at her heels.

Chett grabbed his jeans and shirt from the floor. Questions rolled out one after the other. Questions that pushed his relationship with Cat across the line from fun and games to something dark and, frankly, frightening. *What was that nightmare all about? Is this Cat's life? What have I gotten myself into?*

In the kitchen Catrina handed him a dog biscuit shaped

like a bone, then turned her back on him to fiddle with the coffee machine on the counter.

"I could use some liquid courage." He looked at the fake bone pinched between his thumb and forefinger, looked at Titan sitting expectantly on his haunches a few feet away. The dog's massive head was level with Chett's chest, for crying out loud. Open wide, those jaws would swallow his forearm. He gulped. Sweat ran down his temples.

"There's some red wine left in the living room," she said without turning.

The incentive spurred him to action. He dropped the bone to the floor and used the side of a bare foot to slapshot the biscuit across the tile like a hockey puck on ice.

Titan's conveyor belt of a tongue swept the treat into his cavernous maw. Chett didn't hang around to hear the sharp teeth crunch it to smithereens. He beat a retreat into the living room and flicked on the gas fireplace. Crazy Canucks programmed their energy-saving thermostats for frosty-breath temperatures every night.

Crazy... Catrina's agonized screams still reverberated in his skull.

With a shaking hand he emptied the dregs of the bottle of Italian wine into his and Catrina's abandoned glasses. He picked up his half-filled glass, sipped, sighed, then slugged the rest in a single swallow.

"I opened another bottle. French Merlot. My favorite."

Chett jumped at the sound of Catrina's voice behind him. Despite her attempt at a normal tone, in the firelight and weak light from the kitchen she appeared pale, shattered. He took the bottle from her and filled his glass to the brim.

Before he could drain it, she faced him defiantly. "I scared you."

"You both scared me," he corrected. "Our threesome—

you, me, Titan—sure has its highs and lows. As well as"—he waggled his brows—"superior ins and outs."

"Don't joke." In the firelight her eyes glistened with tears.

He swallowed a mouthful of the wine, reluctantly placed his glass on the coffee table, and sank into the sofa. "Sit with me."

"Please," he added when she turned away, emotion crimping her lips.

She ignored her glass beside his, and complied. He pulled a quilt from the spine of the sofa and tugged her close. Her body felt boneless, as if all the fight inside had taken a hike and wasn't planning on a return trip. He maneuvered her limp upper body across his lap and against his chest under the quilt. It seemed natural to hold Cat with her head nestled in the hollow between his neck and shoulder. He felt her fast heartbeat, sensed the throat tight with explanations she dared not speak. He held her quietly until the beat slowed to a normal rhythm.

"I'm so ashamed," she said into his neck.

"Of what?"

"You saw me like…like…*that*."

"Who else knows about your nightmares?"

"No one. I should be strong enough to handle this."

"We all should be a lot of things we aren't," he said equitably. "I can't handle a dog phobia. Why do you expect more of yourself?"

She remained silent.

[♫ "Lean on Me"]

Long minutes later, he broke the silence. "I don't have the answers, Kitten, but I can listen. Tell me the story."

She rocked her wet cheek against his neck in unspoken refusal. Brad had told Chett that Catrina never spoke to her Port Carson friends about her past. Fear of being judged or pitied or talked about—or perhaps something else—kept her from exposing her history in the fishbowl community to which she'd fled to build a new life.

"I'm a temporary visitor here, remember? I'm not going to reveal your secrets to the locals. I promise you'll feel better after telling someone. Who better than me?"

She took a shuddering breath. "I was a certified scuba diver with the Toronto Police Marine Unit for three years before...before moving here." Her voice broke. "I can't do it. I don't want to go there."

"Step back a little. Describe the memory as if you're watching a movie. Be an observer." He rubbed her back. "I'm here for you. Trust me."

"I'll try." She tucked one arm around his waist and gripped it hard. "The unit gets a tip on the radio early one summer morning from a fisherman out on Lake Ontario. He's spotted a small oil slick two miles offshore. He supplies the GPS coordinates. It's on the Canadian side of the lake. No boat has been reported missing, no distress signal was received. My...the officer in charge calls the team together anyway. We...*they*...put on drysuits, assemble the gear, take the dive boat out."

"Go on."

"It's really choppy. Fifty-mile-per-hour wind gusts. It's lucky the fisherman spotted the slick before it dissipated. There's not much debris floating on the surface to indicate—" A wet sob escaped.

He rubbed her shoulder.

"Me and my partner...," she began, then stopped.

"The two divers," he encouraged.

"The two divers slowly descend one hundred eighty feet, almost the limit. That's about eighteen stories down. It's dark, but they have powerful headlamps and search lights. They spot the mast first, and the sail is furled on the boom. The crew must have been motoring across the lake in the dead of night to avoid border security. Stupid. The divers follow the mast to a thirty-five-foot sailboat laying on its side. The hull near the engine compartment is blown out by an explosion. It must've sunk within minutes. The divers search the boat. The lifeboat is gone. The door to the cabin has a steel bar padlocked across it. The safety diver lowers a crowbar."

Under the hand stroking her back, Chett felt her muscles stiffen, a sure signal that whatever came next wouldn't be good.

"We break open the door," she said, abandoning the effort to keep the story impersonal. "I go in first, shine the light forward into the galley. I see pinpoints of reflected light. Initially I think they're fish eyes. Then I realize the light is reflecting off the corneas of drowned teenage girls. They're floating, long black hair streaming. Arms and legs tangled every which way, filling the cabin." She choked. Violent sobs rattled her lungs.

Chett held on while she cried out the pent-up trauma. Hot tears dripped off his chin into her hair. His tears. "I'm so sorry," he whispered through a thickened throat.

Long minutes later, she resumed. "I have my mask on, air regulator in my mouth. I can't scream, but I want to scream. We recover twelve undocumented Mexican teens, likely destined for prostitution, most of them under fifteen years old. When the engine exploded and the sailboat started to take on water, the bastards abandoned those kids in the cabin to drown. The portholes were too small to allow escape."

Most of Chett's adult life he'd written guns-and-gore action screenplays involving violence, crime, and murder. In the entertainment industry, victims were pawns. Fans of the original *Star Trek* television series called them "red shirts"—bit players destined to die in the show.

Writers deliberately ensured that viewers made emotional connections with the stars of the movies, not the victims. From the little he'd read about PTSD, he'd learned that emotional reactions often triggered long-term trauma in first responders and members of the military. Only a psychopath would indefinitely remain unaffected by tragedy. His movies had no heart, Cat had insisted. She was correct. Action movie screenwriters didn't want the carnage to traumatize viewers. They wanted to stimulate excitement and adrenaline, not heartbreak.

Catrina interrupted his thoughts. "When I close my eyes to try to sleep I see those glowing eyes, the expressions of horror on those pretty girls' faces. I scream at night, I know I do. Titan licks my face, tries to wake me."

Chett managed to croak past the lump in his throat, "Were the human traffickers captured?"

"No."

She hadn't received closure. Meanwhile she suffered. "Have you received therapy?" In California everyone he knew was in therapy.

"I'll work it out myself. It takes time, that's all." She sat up and scrubbed tears from her cheeks with both fists.

Her pain was palpable, raw. Yet she'd been living in Port Carson for a while. "How long has it been since…the event?"

There was a pause. "Two years."

"Two years is a long time to have nightmares reliving that dive."

"Like I said, it takes time."

He leaned to gently kiss her forehead, then her lips. "You and Titan, both of you trained to serve and protect, yet here you are sitting on the sideline in cottage country.

Leaving your job in the Marine Unit didn't solve the problem, did it? My poor darling."

She pushed away from his chest. "I choose how to live my life." Deep-seated pain flashed into defiance.

She swung her legs over and lurched off the sofa. The quilt dropped from her shoulders, and she yanked tight the belt on her robe. Her curvy, statuesque figure, backlit by flickering firelight, left him breathless.

Better he left her alone to sleep, he chastised himself. He had some thinking to do, and Cat was worn out physically and emotionally. "Do you want me to leave?"

"No," she said in a small voice.

"Let's get some shut-eye," he suggested.

On their way to the bedroom he spied Titan curled on a blanket on the kitchen floor, fast asleep. It dawned on him that he'd completely forgotten about the dog.

At the door to Catrina's room, Chett stopped to inspect the damaged doorframe and useless lock. Shrugging his shoulders, he walked through and left the door wide open.

***

Catrina's smartphone burbled. Groggily she reached for the phone and peered at the screen. Eight o'clock already! Secure in Chett's arms when they'd returned to bed following the nightmare and its aftermath, she'd slept soundly for the first time in months.

The caller identified himself. Shocked to her toes, she swung rubbery legs over the edge of the bed and straightened to attention. "Yes, sir?"

On the opposite side of the bed Chett grumbled, "Who is it at this hour on a Sunday morning?"

She placed a hand over the phone's microphone. "It's an OPP sergeant." After a brief one-sided conversation, she said crisply, "I'll be there in under an hour."

She disconnected and relayed to Chett the gist of the conversation. "A snowmobile went through lake ice last night. Their Underwater Search and Recovery dive team needs my help to recover the body."

CHAPTER 15

Danger, Will Robinson

"I'm needed on the dive," Catrina repeated as she dug through a bureau drawer for thermal long underwear. "Only two OPP divers are available today. Without a certified safety diver, they'll have to delay the recovery until one of their other divers is available. That could take another day."

Behind her, Chett pulled on his jeans. "What happened?"

Stick to the facts. Don't think about the dead guy on the bottom of Lake Muskoka. "Early this morning a dog walker discovered a man frozen stiff beside a big hole in the lake ice. He was apparently with another man, who is presumed drowned."

"You sure you're up for this?"

Underwear in hand, Catrina paused on her way to the shower. "I've kept up my certification. I have the training and experience."

"That's not what I meant, and you know it."

"I won't have to go *in* the water." She crossed her fingers out of his sight. "The other divers will recover the body." *They'll bring him up in a body bag. I'll never see his eyes.*

Chett approached from behind and wrapped his arms around her waist. "Why is this so important to you?"

In a clipped tone devoid of emotion—her cop voice—she responded, "Bob, the assistant manager at Tim Hortons, never returned home last night."

Chett stiffened. "My *Mafia Massacre* fan? He's just a kid."

"His mom Muriel and I curl in the same mixed league. She needs confirmation it's her son. The family needs closure. I have to go." *Otherwise, how can I live with myself? I can't be responsible for making them wait longer than necessary.*

He swiveled her to face him and wrapped her in a protective hug. "You don't *have* to do anything. Not after—"

"Last night? That was nothing new," she said bitterly into his chest. "I'm used to the nightmares."

"I'm not," muttered Chett into her hair.

Catrina pulled away. "What's that?"

"Nothing. I'm coming with you." His eyes flashed with determination.

She pushed him away. "Not necessary. I can do this."

"I believe you. I am also aware of how emotionally difficult a body retrieval will be, especially someone we know."

"I should *never* have told you about the…that incident."

"Too late now." In a low voice he entreated, "Listen, I understand how frightened you are and I'm going to be there for you, figuratively holding your hand. Got that?"

"No doubt watching a recovery will be useful research for a guns and gangs screenwriter," the cynical cop in her snapped.

Chett blanched. "Low blow."

"Sorry. Do what you want. You'll have to follow in another vehicle." Frankly, a recovery dive scared her to the tips of her icy fingers and toes. Chett's presence would calm her, ground her, but he wasn't to know that.

She heard him say, "I have your back," as she slammed and locked the bathroom door.

[♬ "Faith"]

***

After feeding Titan and taking him for a short walk, Catrina filled a thermos with strong coffee. Titan would be fine in his kennel. The temperature hovered just below freezing and promised to hold, although the Weather Network app on her phone warned of wet snow or freezing rain. Chett carried a duffel bag with her drysuit, mask and fins to her SUV.

"Here's the address to plug into your GPS in case you lose me," she said.

"Cop driving," he nodded.

She laughed to cover her nervousness. "I'm not a cop, remember? I can get ticketed like anyone else."

He wrapped his arms around her bulky parka and kissed her warmly. "For luck. You can do this."

"Of course I can." *As long as I don't have to go into the water.*

Twenty minutes later Catrina halted at the entrance to a single-lane driveway, waiting on a pickup with a snowplow blade making a turn onto the highway. She waved to Gerry Cousineau as he drove by. Many cottagers, including her clients, hired him to clear their lanes in winter and spread fresh gravel in summer.

The lane meandered for half a mile before a 1930s-era white clapboard cottage with green trim came into view. A decrepit boathouse hugged a shoreline cleared of trees decades before environmental protection regulations. She parked at the tail end of a ribbon of police vehicles and an unmarked van. Chett pulled in behind her.

A group of about twenty locals stood behind a perimeter caution tape strung between a tree and snow-buried Muskoka chairs. Catrina approached the female OPP officer responsible for controlling the small crowd and introduced herself.

"I'm Catrina Turner. Sergeant Wong asked me to assist the dive team."

"My name's Tara Stothers." The tall, red-haired woman removed a heavy glove and gave Catrina's hand a shake. "You're the Toronto ex-cop with the police service dog. I heard about the incident at the Port Carson carnival yesterday."

"News travels fast."

"Videos and photos of Titan performing the rescue are all over Twitter and Facebook. He's famous!" The cop turned to Chett. "Sir, you'll have to stay behind the tape with the others. Please respect the family's privacy and keep your smartphone in your pocket."

Tara escorted Catrina inside the single-story building. A handsome Asian-Canadian man in his forties sat at a kitchen table overlooking the flat expanse of snow-covered lake. He'd kept his parka on in the unheated room. Steel grey threaded thick, dark hair. His smile was welcoming, his eyes appraising.

He half-rose from the chair and extended his hand. "You must be Turner. Ben Wong. I'm the officer in charge on this shift. Glad you could join us."

Catrina recognized his voice from the phone call. "Good to meet you, sir." She squared her shoulders, blew out the anxiety, ignored the acidic coffee churning in her stomach.

After shaking the sergeant's hand, she glanced into the living room, surveying the unlit cast iron wood stove, pine paneling, curling vinyl sheet flooring, sagging sofas, and bookshelves stuffed with old board games and dog-eared paperbacks. The old summer cottage had probably been in the family for generations. Ironically, the peninsula of land it sat on was likely worth close to a million bucks.

Noticing her interest, the sergeant explained, "The owners have allowed us to use their place as a command post."

Tara filled her thermos from a Tim Hortons insulated carton on the counter beside a box of doughnuts. "Donated by Tims in town," she said. "Help yourself." The screen door squealed on rusty hinges as she left to return to her post.

In tragic circumstances, communities rally to support their own. Catrina too had a small but vital part to play. She stared out the front window at a figure on the lake wearing a bright orange flotation jacket and wielding a chainsaw. He cut away jagged edges to create a large triangular hole in the ice. Despite her Arctic-rated down parka, she shivered.

"Have a seat," Sergeant Wong said, indicating the chair opposite his. "Here's the story. The snowmobile went through the ice thirty feet from the shore, as you can see. It's twelve feet under the ice to a sandy bottom. The thaw weakened the lake ice. Our area has seen four fatalities since Friday." He fixed intelligent brown eyes on her. "I hear that you prevented a fifth yesterday. Good work. That's why I called you after waking up your former Toronto Marine Unit sergeant early this morning. Johnson highly recommends you, by the way, and says hello."

Catrina covered an involuntary spasm of fear with a crisp nod. *Wong's not judging me. He doesn't know.* Intractable anxiety dogged her daily that her PTSD had become common knowledge. Back then she'd been too stubborn—or too broken—to tell her sergeant the truth about why she was resigning. In the two years since, she'd battled to regain what she lost. She'd made several recreational dives. She'd paid for police-approved public safety and deep water dive training recertification tests and aced them. This was an opportunity to get back in the game. *I'm ready for this.*

A terrified part of her psyche screamed, *You rescued a dummy for each test, not a drowned man.*

"Glad you can help us out today. My excellent clerk has the paperwork ready." Sergeant Wong slid a few pages of printed text across a wood tabletop scarred with dozens of initials. "It's a one-day civilian contract. Standard rate. Standard waiver."

Catrina studied the contract, noted the hourly rate, and signed her name on two copies with the pen he handed her. He signed, tri-folded his copy and tucked it with the pen into an inside pocket of his parka. Business over, his painted wood chair scraped over the worn floor. "I'll introduce you to the dive team."

They walked across the parking area to a well-trodden path through the snow to the shoreline, and he briskly briefed her on the status of various emergency services personnel called to the scene.

"The volunteer firefighters left on another call. One victim is already at the hospital morgue and we're waiting for autopsy. Hypothermia is the probable cause."

Hypothermia snuck up on drunks. Feeling perversely warm due to the alcohol, they'd doze off outside in frigid temperatures, never to wake up. Almost five percent of Canadian deaths were attributed to cold.

"The body removal people returned for the other victim," Sergeant Wong continued without a break for reply or comment. "They're staying warm in the van. Two uniforms are here to support the dive team. You've met Tara Stothers. Jon Kruse is supervising the cutter widening the hole."

They passed by the members of the public stamping their feet to keep warm behind the caution tape. Chett stuck out an arm and gave her a thumb's up. Warmed by his support, she turned her attention to Muriel Ryerson, Bob's mother, who watched the activity wide-eyed over a gloved hand clamped to her mouth.

Muriel managed the post office. Between Muriel's job and her son's position at Tims, they knew all the cottagers and locals, and everyone knew them. A pale young woman Catrina assumed was Bob's sister or girlfriend gripped Muriel's other hand between bright red mittens. Fat wet snowflakes whitened their fur-trimmed parka hoods. Catrina's heart went out to them but all she could offer was closure, nothing more.

"Meanwhile I'm due at a scene on Georgian Bay." The sergeant continued his one-sided commentary as they trotted down to the shore. "Two men overnighted in a fishing shack with a portable woodstove burning. The hole in the ice caved in, taking them with it." He shook his head sadly. "Climate change. Winter lake ice isn't as thick as it used to be."

Catrina's blood flash froze. *Multiple local fatalities in the icy depths. Will they haunt me too? My nightmares are already close to intolerable.* Coming to the scene had been a *very* bad idea. She fought the urge to flee to her vehicle and drive away as fast as possible from the frozen victim.

[♬ "Cold"]

"We need to wrap up here ASAP because these two divers have to be rested and ready tomorrow for the Georgian Bay dive to sixty feet when our most experienced diver is available. Greg Danson is the team lead on this recovery. You'll report to him. He has an extra suit and equipment for you." He eyed her up and down. "It might be a little large, eh?"

She firmly suppressed blindingly dark fears and refocused on the task. *I can do this.* "I brought my own drysuit, sir."

"Good, good. Here's the rest of the dive team." He introduced her to Danson and Roger Smith, then left.

Danson quizzed Catrina on her winter dive experience. Satisfied, he confirmed that Catrina was to be the backup diver responsible for tending the safety lines attached to the harnesses of the two divers. The unstable ice around the hole rim had been cut away, but they weren't going to chance double human weight on the ice between hole and land. They planned to load the body bag onto a sled. The body removal guys were to drag it ashore by an attached rope. After the operational briefing, Catrina suited up with the others in the cottage but kept her thermal gloves and snow boots on.

Danson and Smith strapped scuba tanks onto their backs, adjusted full-face masks, inserted the regulators into their mouths, and tested the airflow. Finally they pulled on gloves.

Standing on the ice well back, Catrina fed out the lines attached to their harnesses as the two men approached the gaping black triangle in single file, spaced ten feet apart. Danson carried the folded body bag.

When they tipped backward into the water and disappeared, the spectators surged forward, releasing pent-up tension and excitement in a collective buzz.

"Stay behind the caution tape!" Tara ordered.

Catrina maintained laser-focused attention on the lines she held in trembling hands, waiting. When she felt one tug on each of the lines—the divers' signal that everything was okay—she exhaled in relief. *Textbook dive,* she prayed silently. *Nothing will go wrong.*

The seconds, then minutes, ticked by. Snow drifted silently through the grey morning light, blanketing every surface except the ominous black open water. The crowd behind the tape moved restlessly, worried, watching, waiting.

Suddenly three sudden sharp tugs on one line alerted Catrina that a diver intended to surface. A hooded figure broke the flat black water. Catrina approached carefully, braced her legs and extended a hand to assist him onto the ice.

After he yanked off his mask, swear words carried in the still air. "Damn regulator froze."

Although all divers had a second emergency regulator to expand the compressed air in the tanks to a breathable pressure, safety protocol dictated that he end the dive. Her heart hammered under the thick neoprene skin of her suit. *I'm backup.*

Danson tromped across the snow-covered lake in his ungainly fins to shore. Automatically she pulled in his line slack, looping it around her arm. She backtracked to shore behind him, her attention on Smith's line.

"Regulator worked fine yesterday." Danson swore under his breath while shrugging off his tanks and harness and lowering them to a tarp. "We had some trouble lifting the skidoo that pinned him, but he's halfway in the bag." He pointed to the extra tanks, buoyancy compensator, harness, face mask, fins, and regulators and hose nearby. "I can use the spare equipment or you can go in. Your choice."

Danson's grim expression held a challenge, and suddenly she understood what this unexpected offer was about. Danson wanted to observe how she worked a dive. Credentials didn't prove a diver was competent. Rather than take offense, in his place she'd certainly check out a new diver before offering future work on a dive team. Lives were at stake.

She glanced over at Chett, stalwart and supportive, and freezing his California butt off to be figuratively at her side. He modeled courage every time he endured Titan's presence in order to be with her. She mentally heard his voice ask, "Do you want diving work or not?" He'd made it clear he believed she belonged on the force.

But those dead eyes... Panic bubbled under her deceptively calm, controlled expression. Danson expected an immediate decision. Time was of the essence or they'd expose Smith to the unacceptable risk of becoming chilled in the frigid water. It was now or never.

"I'll do it."

CHAPTER 16

Loving someone deeply gives you courage.
– Lao Tzu, philosopher

Catrina dropped backward off the edge of the ice into black water, letting the heavy oxygen tank pull her down. She welcomed the familiar shock that iced her neoprene-covered body. In the early stage of a winter dive, the cold sharpened her senses and her focus. She somersaulted, flicked her fins, and followed Roger Smith's safety line the short distance to lake bottom.

The dull metal hood of a skidoo on its side reflected in the beam of her headlamp. Its handlebars and front skis were twisted skyward as if the driver had made a last-ditch attempt to gun the engine and speed away from the fatally weak ice. Under a starless night sky, with heavy snow falling, they'd stood no chance to detect the danger in time.

The other diver's light illuminated the victim laying face up. Cat's flippers stilled, halting her descent. She stopped breathing when she recognized Bob's round face, now plaster hard with ice-chip, sightless eyes. Her gloved hand hovered beside her safety line, anticipating the onset of out-of-control panic, preparing to signal an end to the dive. *I'm such a mess. Why did I think I could do this?*

To her astonishment, the only emotion she experienced was compassion. *Poor Bob.* Her mind filled with the image of his devastated loved ones attending on the surface, of their faith in the divers to return Bob to them. The pressure of Chett's kiss clung to her lips. Confiding in him had helped. Desolate, dead eyes—or at least, Bob's eyes—had lost their power to destroy her composure. Her breaths in and out maintained a steady rhythm, the familiar bubbles and hiss of the air hose reassuring.

She went to work.

The victim's legs and feet were already inserted into the body bag. His upper body wore a bulky, waterlogged parka. No life vest. With hand signals, Smith indicated that he'd lift the victim while she pulled the bag under the torso. Catrina swam into position and released some air from her flotation jacket until the belt weights anchored her to the sand.

In a minute the victim was zipped and secured. Stationed at each end, holding the handles, the divers inflated their flotation jackets and easily kicked to the triangular opening in the ice, and daylight. Underwater, even a large body weighed no more than thirty-five pounds.

At the hole's edge, Danson pulled the black body bag by a handle onto the waiting sled while Smith pushed. Icy water streamed from the mesh. Holding an attached rope, Danson backtracked to shore.

Catrina and Smith hovered, heads above water, waiting while the body removal people pulled the shed over snow-covered ice to land. Then, sled weight off the lake ice, the male OPP constable wearing an orange flotation jacket hurried to assist the divers out of the water. Catrina rolled away from the opening to distribute her weight, sat up, and exchanged her flippers for snow boots. She took an alternate route to shore in case the weight of the sled had cracked the ice. Smith followed ten feet behind.

Tara unzipped the bag, peered quickly inside, then zipped it closed. Shoulders hunched, head bent, she trudged through the snow to Muriel and the girl. A murmur from the crowd swelled as she lifted the tape and motioned the women to step aside for a private conversation. The locals knew the cops bought their coffees and lunches at Tims. Even if Tara's demeanor hadn't broadcast the confirmation, it was a given that Tara was acquainted with Bob. Catrina's eyes misted. Tara had taken upon herself the most difficult of a cop's duties—to break the tragic news to the family, compounded by her own grief.

The trio of women clustered around one of the Muskoka chairs left at the shore for the winter. Nearby, the officers, the locals, the divers—all stopped whatever they were doing and stood respectfully in thick, falling snow, heads bowed. Several men removed their toques. A cell phone rang and was quickly silenced.

A keen wail shattered the stillness. All hope destroyed, Muriel stumbled in deep snow up the slope to the parking lot. The young woman loudly begged to see for herself and made a beeline for the body bag.

Tara raced after her, caught her arm, and propelled her in the direction of the parked vehicles. "I'll drive you and his mother to the hospital. You'll have the opportunity to say goodbye, I promise, but not here. Not in front of all of these people." Thickening snow muffled the rest of the conversation.

The recovery over, dreaded outcome confirmed, the onlookers shifted in unison in the direction of their parked vehicles. Catrina walked over to Chett.

He reached for her gloved hand. "You doing all right?"

"I'm fine." She squeezed his hand briefly and released it. "I need to change and pack up gear. You go on home."

He attempted to draw her in for a hug, but she resisted, tilting her head toward the members of the public who hung back. "I'm on duty."

He grinned. "So you are. I knew you could do it. Join me at Jenna's for a hot drink when you're free?"

"Will do." For his ears alone she whispered, "Thank you for believing in me."

***

Two hours later, after lunch at Tim Hortons to pay her respects to Bob's colleagues, Catrina stopped at her townhouse to pick up Titan. To her disbelief, Chett hadn't run away after her freakish nightmare. Instead he'd supported her at the scene, had her back. His stalwart confidence had propped up her courage to face her deepest fear. It meant a lot. She wasn't a smooth talker, had always had difficulty expressing her feelings. But she intended to demonstrate to Chett how important his presence had been to her that day. She hummed along to a classic love song on the radio.

[♬ "I Finally Found Someone"]

At the bottom of Jenna's lane, Catrina parked beside the garage and let Titan out for a run. The snow had ceased falling, and weak sunlight filtered through gaps in the cloudcover. Titan's enormous snout sniffed the air before he bounded joyously across the expanse of fresh snow, heading for the trees and the wildlife cached within. Freedom!

Feeling at peace for the first time in a *very* long time, she watched Titan until he disappeared behind a curtain of sagging snowy branches. After that terrible dive in Lake Ontario, the effects of debilitating trauma had squelched all remnants of such unabashed, pure joy in her own heart. Fear and pain had so dominated her existence she couldn't even separate and identify the mixed emotions tumbling inside her in that moment. Sorrow for Bob? Relief that she'd conquered her deepest fear? Hope for the future? Gratitude?

I love that dog. She stretched out her arms. *I love my life.*

Chett opened the door. He was attired in an unzipped parka and wearing the cowboy boots that reminded her of Big Joe. Dimples bracketed an eager smile. Her heart leaped. *I love those dimples.*

He carefully walked across the ice-rutted driveway to where she stood and gave her a quick peck on the lips. Too quick.

Her eyes narrowed. "What's up?"

"Come in," he invited. "Titan will be all right for a few minutes outside?"

A few minutes?

Then she spied the luggage on the porch by the door. It could only mean one thing. Her elation at seeing him drained into her snow boots.

"I had a call from Jenna," he explained. "Last night at a party she convinced an important producer to listen to our pitch. We have a follow-up meeting tomorrow afternoon in L.A. I called a limo service to drive me to the Toronto airport. It's due to arrive any minute." He pulled Catrina in for an exuberant hug, but there was nothing intimate about it. "This is my big break! I want to tell you all about it."

A black four-door sedan rolled down the driveway like an ominous dark cloud and pulled up. The driver popped the trunk.

"Damn. No time. My ride's here." Chett kissed her, released her. "Sorry, Kitten, I'm already cutting it close. I have to hurry." He dug into his jeans pocket and pulled out the house keys. "Can you put these back in Jenna's hiding place?"

Catrina stuck out a gloved hand, palm up. *So this is what it comes down to: a kiss and a key handover.*

"I'll call you from L.A.," he promised as the driver loaded the luggage into the trunk.

Sure you will. She wasn't holding her breath. She believed, even if Chett wasn't ready to admit it, that his few weeks in Canada would soon only be a fun memory, especially now that he had industry people to meet, deals to make, pages to write. Stinging tears breached the crumbling dam of her self-control. *I knew he'd leave eventually. What's the matter with me?*

With a wave, Chett slid into the back seat and slammed the door. The driver made a three-point turn and accelerated up the lane. In seconds Chett was out of sight. Out of her life.

[♬ "Goodbye My Lover"]

It was her responsibility to close up Jenna's lake house for the remainder of the winter. As the afternoon light faded to black—like her love life—she decided to deal with the necessary mundane housekeeping tasks immediately. A welcome distraction.

She closed a finger over the house keys in her palm for each task: *book a cleaning service to clean and do the laundry, call the plumber to drain and winterize the water lines—*

A tear rolled down her cheek and dripped onto her glove. She forced herself to concentrate. Third finger—*restock the pantry, freezer, and wine cellar with dry goods, frozen protein, and alcohol, respectively—*

Tears gushed. She curled the little finger. *Take Jenna's vehicle to a garage for maintenance, and*—thumb—*remove all evidence of the guest's occupancy.*

The waterfall of tears blurred her vision. *It's not like you were falling in love or anything. Shake it off, Turner!*

She whistled for Titan and let him lead the way into the lake house. After toeing off her boots, she pulled her phone out of her parka pocket and speed-dialed the plumber. No answer. She left a message. The cleaning woman's voicemail informed callers, "We're on a beach in Mexico until the fifteenth."

Heaving a tremulous sigh, Catrina decided that cleaning an unoccupied house could be delayed a couple of weeks as long as she removed trash that might attract rodents. She snagged a green garbage bag from the utility room and methodically emptied the wastebaskets in every room. Titan sprawled on the hearth of the cold, ash-filled fireplace to wait.

In Jenna's study she pulled several sheets of crumpled paper out of a wicker basket under the printer table. *Note to self: add printer paper to the shopping list.*

She was about to dump the contents of the basket into the green plastic bag when the word "diver" on the top sheet caught her eye. She dropped everything and smoothed the paper flat on Jenna's desk. With volcanic horror she read...

Sunk

© Chett de Groot

A by-the-book FBI investigator who is terrified of water teams with a sexy diver with attitude on a human trafficking case in the Florida Keys. When his female partner and love interest is kidnapped and held as collateral to guarantee safe passage of underage girls destined for prostitution, the protagonist must learn love conquers fear before more women end up at the bottom of the ocean.

Her breathing rate ratcheted into overdrive. Catrina retrieved and smoothed another crumpled page. Chett had summarized each key scene in separate paragraphs.

They involved high-speed boat chases, gun battles, and sex between the hero and heroine.

She unfolded another discarded piece of paper, scanned the contents, and her leg bones softened, noodled, until she knelt on the floor. An anguished gasp seared her throat. He'd written a paragraph about the discovery of dead teenage girls floating in the locked cabin of a sunken sailboat. *He promised he wouldn't betray my secret.*

Swiftly she dumped the contents of the wicker basket on the hardwood floor and methodically flattened each piece of paper. Soon the history of his writing efforts during his stay in Muskoka lay spread out on the maple planks. He'd scribbled revisions on several iterations of *Kingpin of the Sea*, an action screenplay treatment, as well as drafts of the scripts for *Lust in Space* and *The Seduction of Miss Prudence Maxwell.*

She picked out a single-page scene outline for *Kingpin of the Sea*. It did *not* include the underwater sailboat scene in the list.

So that's what he'd been doing in the hours after he left the Lake Muskoka recovery dive that morning—typing up the description of her nightmare. "Describe the memory as if you're watching a movie," he'd coaxed. "Trust me."

The bastard.

Fury warred with shame, with outrage. Chett had lied about being at the recovery dive to support her. His screenplay came first. *He exploited me, and my...my problem.* With shaking fingers, she savagely ripped the pages into tiny pieces. "I *hate* him."

CHAPTER 17

Game Over

Six weeks later, Catrina opened the door to the SereniTea Shoppe and strolled in, Titan at her heels. The four elderly women enjoying afternoon tea ignored Titan. His nails clicked on the hardwood floor as he passed them and trotted through open French doors to the balcony. He immediately dropped and sprawled on his side on the bare wood warm from the afternoon March sunshine.

A soggy wedge of snow tobogganed down the shop's metal roof and plopped onto Titan's tail. He scrambled to his feet and wagged it frantically to shake the snow off. Catrina chuckled. Laughing felt good. It had been a while.

The previous evening, a late snowfall had dumped four inches of sparkling snow. Although eager to share her news with Brigit, Cat remained at the railing, soaking up the sun and lake view. Ice receded from the shores of Lake Muskoka. The city dwellers would descend in the coming weekends to open up their cottages, float their docks, and repair winter damage from wind and wildlife.

Every spring the local stores, resorts, campgrounds, marinas, golf courses, and service providers finalized their choices to fill summer jobs. Even the Ontario Provincial Police added seasonal staff to deal with the influx of thousands of visitors, many of whom got themselves into trouble on and in the water. Catrina had gathered her courage and submitted an application. It was a big step, but she felt ready. The nightmares woke her only once or twice a week these days. She'd been invited to fill in on two other OPP team dives, and hadn't freaked out, which bolstered her fragile confidence.

I really can do this.

When she told Brigit about the job application, her friend had briskly observed, "It's about time." Catrina had never shared her struggles with nightmares or the battle to heal from her past experiences, but she suspected that Brigit knew all along that Cat suffered from PTSD.

In the weeks following Chett's departure, Catrina's internal trauma continued to loosen its grip. Instead of being mired most days in her own emotional struggles and exhaustion from lack of sleep, her attention had turned outward. She focused more on other people. Cat belatedly discerned that Brigit was empathic as well as intelligent. The talented baker and pastry chef understood people on a deep level, much like those amateur detectives in the cozy mystery novels she devoured.

Frankly, in Cat's decade as a cop she'd never wasted valuable time on the twisted motivations that drove individuals to break the law. Maybe that was why she'd never made detective. Brigit, on the other hand, loved to psychoanalyze.

Hey, I bet Brigit broke up with good old boy-next-door Brad because he, not the sex, bored her. Made sense that Brigit had wanted to get her floury hands on Chett, an interesting stranger.

Catrina reluctantly stepped out of the warm sun to join her friend. Inside, Brigit stood behind the carrara marble-topped counter. She loaded a tray with a teapot, two cups and saucers, and a white wicker basket filled with fresh scones. She wore a frilly white apron over a blue cotton dress that matched her eyes. Very 1950s. Tourists and the retired four-season cottagers lapped up the nostalgia.

Catrina carried the tray over to a coffee table at the rear of the tearoom, out of earshot of the gossip grannies.

She poured two cups of peppermint tea, placed a warm cranberry scone on her saucer, and sank with a sigh into a chintz-covered armchair. Brigit settled into the chair opposite and picked up her teacup.

Hungry, Catrina opened her mouth to bite into the flaky scone just as the cell phone in her fleece pocket rang. She pulled it out, checked the caller ID, then swiped *Cancel*.

Brigit *tutt-tutted*. "It's Chett again?" As if she needed an answer.

Catrina frowned. "You'd think he'd have given up by now."

"He's been calling and texting you for weeks," Brigit murmured. "Maybe he has important news?"

"I don't want to hear about his f—" She bit off the swear word. "Screenplay. He's left Muskoka for good. Our... *relationship* is over. I've moved on."

Brigit tipped her head of blond curls to one side, plucked brows raised, mascaraed eyelashes batting significantly. Brigit was a girly-girl. "To whom, exactly?" When Catrina merely glared, she sighed. "Have you considered that he might miss you, that he has feelings for you?"

"He got what he wanted from me," Catrina growled. This was well-trod ground. Brigit just wouldn't leave it alone. Cat abruptly changed the subject. With inflated enthusiasm, she announced her news. "This morning I signed a five month contract with the OPP! I start patrolling the District of Muskoka's inland water in May."

Brigit leaned forward and patted her knee. "That's wonderful! Congratulations!"

"It's a start. If all goes well, my contract will be renewed for the winter season to patrol the snowmobile-trail network."

With a silver butter knife, Brigit spread butter on her scone. "What about your clients?"

"I plan to hire a student in a community college security program." Catrina set her empty teacup down and braced her elbows on her knees. "As for what I'll do if the Bracebridge detachment eventually offers me a full-time position, well, I'll worry about what to do with Turner and Pooch Security Services then."

"What about Titan? You aren't going to leave him at home all day?"

"I suggested to the sergeant that Titan and I do some campground and park talks. For example, I proposed to hand out sterile gauze pads and freezer bags, and teach parents how to prepare scent preservation kits in case their kids get lost."

"Sniff kits?" Brigit buttered a second scone. Apparently she'd abandoned her latest diet.

"Yeah. The parent swipes the kid's armpit and stores the pad in a sealed baggie in a suitcase or, if at home, in a sealed jar at room temperature. Then if the child gets lost while hiking or playing, a trained dog such as Titan can track it easily."

"Great idea," Brigit mumbled around a mouthful of the scone.

"The sergeant thought so. My suggestion may have sealed the deal, so to speak."

"Catrina—" Brigit hesitated.

"What is it?" Internally Cat groaned. Brigit had a one-track mind. Catrina didn't have to be a detective to deduce she hadn't been successful in derailing Brigit's train of thought.

"Chett's been so persistent. Why won't you at least read his texts or listen to the voicemails before deleting them?"

Catrina recoiled from admitting the truth. Her fury in regards to Chett's exploitation of her traumatic dive in his screenplay had subsided with time and logic—it'd be years before the film appeared in theaters, if ever. No local movie watcher, even Chett's fans, could possibly connect the scene, or Chett, with the Canadian sailboat incident that had triggered her PTSD.

In an emotionally fragile state she'd fallen fast and hard for that rattlesnake, resulting in a shattered, battered heart that intensified the nightmares that plagued her. She had no intention of corresponding with Chett and poking awake more horrible pain. Shutting him out was her only option. "He'll give up eventually," was all she said.

"Catrina." Disappointment pulled down the corners of Brigit's rosebud mouth. "You're hiding from Chett. It's not right." Frustrated, she threw her pink-tipped fingers up in the air. "It's not brave. What happened to the courageous woman who rescued tiny Lilly?"

Catrina rolled her eyes. "Titan retrieved the child. All I—"

Brigit crossed her arms. "How often does Chett call? Tell me, who is making an effort? Not you!" The expression on Catrina's face must have spoken volumes, because Brigit continued softly, compassionately, "What are you afraid of?"

"You don't understand," Catrina managed to say despite the lump in her throat.

"Agreed. I do not understand why you are blowing off a hot guy who is really into you. Tell me, and I'll let it go."

"May I remind you that he lives in California? He's American. There's no future for us."

Triumphant, Brigit lifted a forefinger. "Aha! So you *have* thought about it. Do I really need to remind you that Canadians and Americans marry so they can live in each other's country permanently?"

"Marriage?" Catrina scoffed. "We, ah, dated for not

even two weeks. Ships passing in the night, and all that. I'm only a notch on his belt. He doesn't belong here." *He stirs up too many emotions.* "I'm better off without him."

"So you're saying he's a fish out of water? It's the end of the road? Water under the bridge? Onward and upward?" Amusement crinkled the corners of Brigit's blue eyes, belying her deadpan expression.

"I don't have time for this." Catrina stood. "Come, Titan," she commanded loud enough to carry to the balcony.

"Hold on. I'm sure I can come up with more clichés," Brigit teased. "All washed up? A good man is hard to find? Or rather, a hard man is good to find?" She waggled her eyebrows.

"Game *over*."

"You're no fun," Brigit pouted.

"Titan and I have rounds to finish. We'd better get a move on. Please add the tea and scones to my tab."

"A faint heart never a true love knows," Brigit called out to Cat's back as she beat a retreat, dog in tow.

Catrina stiffened, then marched on. That jibe hit an unhappy nerve. She refused to give Brigit the satisfaction of knowing she'd scored.

***

That evening in her kitchen, Catrina cut a cooked chicken breast into thin slices to top the romaine lettuce in her salad. Titan sat expectantly on his haunches. Drool dripped onto the floor mat.

"You're retired, Titan, so I guess it's okay to spoil you." She palmed a slice. "Shake a paw."

Titan obediently lifted a paw.

She shook it, said "Good boy," and tossed the piece of chicken. "That's your third treat. The rest is for me. Lie down."

His massive head drooping, Titan ambled the few steps to his blanket on the floor and settled in, snout on front paws, to watch for food that might accidentally fall on the floor.

Catrina's cell phone rang, unusual for that time of night. She checked the caller ID before accepting the call. "Hello?"

"Turn on your television," demanded Brigit with excitement. "Guess who's on *Entertainment Tonight*?"

Catrina grabbed the remote off a side table and switched to the cable channel Brigit indicated. The flat-screen brightened. A familiar *ET* hostess held a microphone to Jenna Jordan, stunning in a red dress and heels, standing beside Chett outside the gates of a major Hollywood film studio.

Chett's image jump-started Cat's heart. He looked tanned and fit in an open-neck white shirt with sleeves rolled up, worn jeans, and his beat-up cowboy boots. *Even after all these weeks, the sight of him arouses feelings best left undisturbed.*

She sank onto her sofa to watch. Of its own volition, her finger pressed *Record* so she could torment herself by watching the segment over and over.

"Jenna," the hostess continued the interview, "tell us more about the development deal with producer Richard Cairncross. Are you attached to the action film?"

Jenna possessively wrapped her arm around Chett's waist and tucked her expertly styled head into the crook of his neck. "Chett de Groot is writing a wonderful lead role for me."

The hostess's eyes widened. "Are you two back together?" Candid beach shots flashed onscreen of a younger Jenna, boobs falling out of a bikini, lip-locked to Chett in surfing shorts.

Chett and Jenna? Catrina doubled over to contain the pain searing her soul. Tears threatened, and she scrunched her eyes to lock them down. *I refuse to be jealous. To care.*

The segment cut to Chett and Jenna at the studio gate for another sound bite. Chett leaned into the microphone. "This film will raise awareness of human trafficking for prostitution. It's a serious issue that deserves international attention."

Jenna nodded. "The United Nations has asked me to be a spokesperson."

"Who does Jenna think she is," Catrina muttered morosely. "Angelina Jolie?"

"I never guessed Jenna Jordan and Chett were an item," Brigit said in her ear.

Catrina jumped. She'd forgotten she held the cell phone. "An item?" Her voice scraped a throat raw with misery.

"As in lovers. Makes sense now that Jenna loaned him the use of her lake house, carte blanche."

The brightly smiling hostess turned her back on the entwined, beaming couple and wrapped up the interview. "You heard it first here, folks. Jenna Jordan will star in *Sunk*. Watch for it at the Sundance and Cannes festivals in a couple of years. It's sure to be another Cairncross blockbuster."

Catrina clicked off the television.

"Did Chett mention his relationship with Jenna?" Brigit persisted.

"He wouldn't, would he?" Catrina admitted reluctantly. "He wanted a fling, no strings. We both did. What happens in Muskoka stays in Muskoka."

"Then why does he keep calling you?"

"To apologize?" *That must be it.* "He's a two-timing jerk."

"You don't sound convinced. Talk to him. Find out."

"Gotta go," Catrina deflected. "See you tomorrow for our afternoon break, as usual." Before Brigit could detect emotion in Cat's voice, she hung up.

Catrina dropped the phone and buried her face in her palms. The wall she'd built to imprison her violent emotions collapsed, allowing great heaving sobs to escape. At her shoulder, Titan whined and licked her hands, offering solace.

She'd convinced herself that fun and games were all she wanted from Chett.

She'd convinced herself that she was *relieved* he'd returned to Hollywood.

But her stubborn heart was never convinced. Cat was forced to acknowledge an indisputable fact: she'd fallen in love with the duplicitous screenwriter.

[♬ "Stone Cold"]

CHAPTER 18

Spring Thaw

April runoff had gouged deep ruts into Jenna's laneway. Catrina was so focused on maneuvering over them as she drove down the slope that she failed to notice the late-model sedan parked behind the garage, its trunk open, until she braked.

"What's this, Titan? Another unannounced guest?" Catrina groused to the dog in the back seat. Yet again Jenna's assistant had failed to inform Catrina in advance so that she could ensure the lake house was ready. She pulled out her phone to dial the woman in California.

With a finger poised over the call button, she heard a door slam. A familiar figure strode across the porch and across the pea gravel in her direction.

Chett de Groot.

"What the—" Her heart battered her ribs, and she swore under her breath. "I never expected to see *him* here again." Titan's menacing growl magnified the consternation rattling her voice, her nerves, her hard-won peace.

As he approached the driver's door, Cat remained behind the wheel, fighting a chicken-hearted impulse to reverse the SUV and hightail it up the lane to the main road. *He's Jenna's guest. It's my job to welcome him.*

She rolled down the window. What do you say to a former lover who'd moved on, and you hadn't? Her stomach flipped like a gymnast in the Olympics.

A couple of feet from the vehicle, serious blue eyes stared into hers. Dimples were nowhere to be found in cheeks sporting a couple days' sandy stubble.

"Shut off the engine, Catrina, and come in the house. We need to talk."

She switched off the engine but didn't make a move to exit the vehicle. "Is Jenna inside?" she asked finally.

His brows flew to his hairline, as if he had not expected that question. "No. I'm alone—*we're* alone. I've been trying to call. I was worried."

Pain pinched wan features. He was hurt, she intuited. But hey, she hurt more. "You left me," she blurted.

"I left messages. Dozens, maybe hundreds."

The soul-deep pain of betrayal erupted from the deep place it had been buried. "You stole my story of those trafficking deaths for your screenplay."

The accusation had the effect of a slap. His upper body recoiled, but he held his ground. "The word *stole* is rather harsh. I prefer *inspired*. I've been trying to explain and give you this." He reached into his leather jacket's inside pocket and pulled out an envelope. He handed it to her through the open window. "It's a check for ten thousand dollars."

She ripped open the envelope. It indeed contained a check from a major studio made out in her name. Suspicion clawed her insides. She'd been a cop for too long to believe in gifts of cash in return for nothing. "What's this, hush money to buy me off so I don't sue the studio?"

His eyes narrowed. "Hey, there's no copyright on ideas," he shot back. "You wouldn't have a case."

She waved the check at him. "Then what's the money for?"

He stepped up to the vehicle and leaned in, one arm along the window frame. "Because it's the moral thing to do. It's payment for partial story credit for *Sunk*. Mickey McNichol, my agent, negotiated your compensation as part of my development deal."

Titan thrust his head between the front seats, over Catrina's shoulder and panted. Doggy breath washed her face. Less than a couple of feet away, Chett didn't budge. He continued without a break, practically nose to nose with Catrina. "I had to leave for L.A. before I had a chance to talk to you. However, I intended all along to compensate you for your death-in-a-sailboat-cabin story concept."

"Without my knowledge or agreement." She wasn't letting him buy her off. Just how generous was he anyway? "What percentage does this ten grand represent? How much do *you* get?"

"Two hundred thousand upon delivery of the shooting script against half a million dollars total when the film goes into principal photography. That means I'm paid the balance when financing is locked and the movie goes into production." He paused. "Is *that* why you're mad at me? I couldn't figure out why you didn't return my calls. I thought we'd started something special."

"Mad is an understatement," she said with force, hoping he didn't notice how the hand holding the check shook.

"You felt used?"

More like betrayed. "Don't psychoanalyze me." She accepted that he didn't have to give her a dime in compensation. So he must be trying to get on her good side for another reason. The water supply hookup, perhaps. "How long will you be staying this time?"

"Until September."

"What!"

"RUFF, RUFF, RUFF." Titan's aggrieved barking in her ear echoed her yell. "Quiet, boy. Sit." The dog obeyed and retracted his massive head.

"I bought something for you." Chett yanked open the driver's door and rear door for Titan. "Come on. It's in the trunk of my car."

"*Your* car?" *How can I avoid him for four and a half months?*

He nodded. "I drove here from California."

Jenna, *his girlfriend*, was expected in late June for an eight week holiday. Pain sliced and diced the anger and outrage in Cat's heart. She could handle Chett shacked up with Jenna in California, but Jenna in a barely-there bikini in Chett's arms—or worse, wearing that lizard costume—here in Muskoka... Tears blurred Cat's vision, and she shaded her eyes with a palm. It wasn't fair. Port Carson was a small community. There was no escape.

What the hell's the matter with me? The man betrayed me. I need to put the vehicle in gear and get out of here.

However, Titan took away the choice by leaping from the back seat through the open rear door to the ground. Chett didn't flinch as Titan brushed past him.

Chett walked over to the open trunk, rummaged between suitcases until he found a shopping bag, and returned to hand it to her where she remained seated in her vehicle.

She reached into the bag and pulled out a curved imitation-metal piece of plastic with straps. "What's this?"

"Wonder Woman's forearm cuff." He smirked, so pleased with himself.

Catrina's mouth hung open, at a loss for words.

"Check out the rest of the costume."

She peered into the bag. The headband appeared to be the real thing. "Was this costume used on the film set?"

"I'm not *that* well connected," he laughed. "I found the outfit in a knockoff movie costume shop near Rodeo Drive." He pointed to the website URL printed on the bag. "They have an online store," he added with a significant lilt to his voice.

She didn't understand. "Is this costume to add to Jenna's collection?"

"I bought it for you. You're the bravest woman I know. You *are* Wonder Woman, in service to the public good." She allowed him to grab her elbow, but stiffened. He rushed on, "I should have told you—I mean *asked* you—for your permission, but there was no time. I told Jenna about the scene on the phone, and she told Cairncross, and I had to leave for L.A. right away to follow up. Jenna's career was on the line, not to mention mine. I'm sorry if I upset you."

"What about Jenna?"

"What about her?" Now he looked confused. He released her and cocked his head.

"Aren't you two together? I saw you on *Entertainment Tonight*."

He rolled his eyes. "I have no idea why the *ET* producers dug up that ancient footage of me and Jenna. It dates from before my marriage. Jenna and I are long-time friends. We're like this"—he entwined his forefinger and second finger. "Not like"—he circled his forefinger and thumb, and pumped the other forefinger in and out of the hole—"this."

Despite herself, she smiled. To give herself time to process heart-expanding relief, she waved a hand at the dog seated in the wet grass nearby, watchful. "Why aren't you afraid of Titan?"

He shrugged. "Obviously if we're to have any chance at a relationship, I had to deal with my dog phobia. I told myself that if you can face your worst fear, so can I. I made appointments with two L.A. psychologists and a hypnotist before I got lucky with a licensed therapist who used energy psychology to cure me of my lifelong fear of dogs."

He had addressed his phobia for her? *Wow.* "Energy psychology? Never heard of it."

"It's also called Emotional Freedom Techniques or EFT. You tap on acupressure points to disconnect the stimulus—in my case dogs—from an emotional reaction."

Catrina snorted. Like most cops, she belonged to the "have to see it to believe it" club of skeptics.

"Yeah, it sounds way out even to this Californian, but I was motivated. I tried one technique after another until I found one that worked for me."

"Do you think it would work on my, ah, nightmares?" Her world opened up a little wider at the possibility of a treatment for her PTSD that didn't involve pouring her guts out and revisiting the experience in talk therapy. The nightmares were bad enough. She put the shopping bag on the passenger seat, got out of the vehicle and walked over to Titan.

"Prove to me that EFT worked for you." She gave Titan the command to stay and crossed her arms. "Pet him," she dared.

Chett ran fingers through his mussed sun-bleached hair. "The knight's challenge to win the hand of the princess? I get it."

"No stalling."

"You're pretty cold-hearted for a princess," he said, tapping various locations on his face with a forefinger.

"What are you doing?"

"Calming myself. The L.A. therapist only had a standard poodle available for my final test. Titan's the size of a bear." Chett blew out a loooong breath. "I'm ready."

He approached the dog and stuck a hand in front of Titan's nose to sniff. "We also worked on dog-handling strategies."

"Certainly helpful," Catrina acknowledged, watching carefully as his hand drifted the length of Titan's side until he bent, closed the gap, and swiped the fur on the hindquarters, as far as possible from Titan's sharp teeth.

He stepped away and raised both arms in victory. "I did it."

"I'm impressed," she said, and meant it. He'd made huge progress in dealing with his phobia. "There might actually be something to this weird tapping thing. Where can I learn it?"

"I'll help you find a qualified therapist. But first, isn't the princess supposed to reward the knight after a successful challenge?"

He stood tall and apparently aloof. Pride kept him from making a move. Her initial rejection had stung. She considered. Chett had dealt with his dog phobia for her. He'd returned to Muskoka to be with her. He'd apologized. What more proof of his sincerity did a girl expect?

She closed the distance between them, wrapped her arms around his waist, tugged him close, and tilted her face up for his kiss. "Let's see where this goes," she whispered.

His tongue reverently traced her eager lips.

"What do I taste like?" she murmured, eyes closed with anticipation.

"You taste like home."

EPILOGUE

Me, Tarzana. You, Big Joe.

"Has Titan's life vest arrived yet?" Catrina leaned on an oil-stained counter inside the wood-framed building of Port Carson Boat Works.

Brad Scott scrolled through the purchase-order log on a tablet mounted on a stand. The wall behind him separated the small retail section from the heart of the business—the workshop where he repaired boat engines. The local men had nicknamed him Scotty, a tip of the hat to mechanical wizardry in the vein of the *Star Trek* engineer played by the late Canadian James Doohan.

The store sold paddles, towropes, buoys, flotation equipment, flags, lightbulbs, engine oil, and other marine supplies. Summer was Scotty's busy season. It was rare to find him in the store.

"Special orders take time." Sweat beaded Scotty's high forehead despite the ceiling fan circulating air that was unusually warm for early June. "Heidi, my clerk, is off for a couple of days to be a bridesmaid at a wedding. I'll have her follow up with the supplier when she returns."

Outside on the marina gas dock, cabin cruisers, a small yacht, a couple of jet boats, and some sleek ski boats queued for fill-ups at the gas pumps in preparation for fishing, waterskiing, tubing, and other water fun that sunny weekend. Catrina's rookie male partner was waiting his turn in the Ontario Provincial Police patrol boat tied up at the end of the wide cedar dock.

Scotty closed the app on the screen, reached into a mini-fridge under the counter, and handed her a cold bottle of water. "Is the dog vest an OPP purchase? You plan on taking Titan on patrol?"

"Thanks," she said, taking the water. "No, it's personal. Titan is officially retired." Sweat trickled down Catrina's spine under her police-issue short-sleeved shirt. She gratefully gulped half the bottle's contents. "We plan on taking him boating this summer. Chett wants to explore the Georgian Bay islands up by Cognashene."

"I explored a few of those deserted, swimsuit-optional islands myself in my youth," Scotty said, winking.

Catrina's cheeks burned. He was onto them. "Any chance you'll share the locations of those deserted islands?"

He opened his mouth, then reconsidered. "Is this a professional or personal interest?" When she hesitated, Scotty chuckled. "You're a cop. No way I'm revealing the younger generation's party locations."

"Drinking and boating don't mix," she remonstrated.

"These days teens bring along tents and sleeping bags and camp out overnight."

Catrina shrugged. "You're a hockey coach and employ summer staff." She nodded through open double doors in the direction of two shirtless, bronzed college students filling customers' tanks. "If anyone knows what these kids are up to, it's you." At least she'd diverted Scotty from the topic of her and Chett's sex life. She dug a wallet out of her shorts pocket. "I'll take a Georgian Bay nautical chart and bottle of water for my partner as well. Ask Heidi to text me when the custom life vest arrives, will you?"

Catrina stepped out from the dark interior and slid the sunglasses on the top of her head into place against the brilliant sunshine. At the end of the wide gas dock she rejoined her partner waiting in the OPP patrol boat.

"Since we have time, I'll pop over to the post office,"

she told him as she handed him the cold bottle of water. "I'll be back in ten."

The Main Street concrete sidewalk radiated heat through the rubber soles of her shoes. She pushed open the drugstore door and gratefully stepped into air-conditioned coolness. The Canada Post outlet was located at the rear of the store.

Muriel Ryerson smiled from behind the counter. "I've been hoping to run into you! I had a letter from the investment firm that manages the Port Carson High School scholarship fund. You donated *ten thousand* dollars toward an annual scholarship in my son's name. I can't believe your generosity." Her brown eyes filled with tears.

"Bob will be remembered at every high school graduation," Catrina affirmed.

Muriel reached across the counter and gripped Catrina's hand. "Thank you," she choked. "But why?"

Catrina expected that Muriel, along with the entire community, wondered how Cat could afford such a large donation on her income. Here was an opportunity to nip speculation in the bud without revealing she'd donated the ten grand that Chett's agent had negotiated on her behalf. Let them think it was a group tribute.

"Did you know that Bob is indirectly responsible for Jenna and Chett's film deal? Bob introduced Chett to Henrik Muller who works for Richard Cairncross, the producer who bought the screenplay."

"The Cairncross who owns Loon Island?"

"That's him. Without Bob's matchmaking, the movie deal never would have happened. Bob was a special person, and he loved movies. Jenna Jordan has offered to present the first scholarship at the June graduation ceremony."

"Oh my gosh." Muriel slapped a palm to her chest. "No kidding? I did hear that Jenna's gonna star in the movie.

I can't thank you all enough." Muriel blew her nose with a tissue. "Now what can I do for you today?"

"I'm picking up a package." Catrina handed over the delivery notice.

Muriel wiped her eyes under her bifocals with a fresh tissue, scrutinized the slip of paper, and disappeared momentarily into the storeroom. She returned with a flat, rectangular box. "Hollywood Costume Emporium," she read off the return label. "Beating the Halloween rush, eh?"

Catrina flushed. "Sure, that's it." She shoulder checked for eavesdroppers. An elderly woman next in line grinned back at her. "Hello, Mrs. Tamilonis." *Great.* One of the sharpest gossiping granny regulars at SereniTea Shoppe.

"Hello, dear." The stooped little woman's pale blue eyes twinkled behind thick glasses.

Catrina sighed. She'd enjoyed more privacy in Toronto, a city of three million people.

"You owe thirty dollars in duty." Muriel tapped the amount into the credit card reader.

Catrina duly inserted a credit card into the handheld unit and tapped in her PIN. At least the two women had no idea what was *in* the box. She tucked the package under one arm and, while she waited for the receipt, imagined Chett's reaction when he saw her in this costume.

***

The morning of Catrina's next day off, she ran a few errands in town while Chett worked on his screenplay, then drove out to Jenna's place with Titan in the back seat, his head angled out a window to catch a breeze. The air above the paved road shimmered in midday heat. Cyndi Lauper's hit "Girls Just Want to Have Fun" blasted from the MP3 player through the vehicle's speakers, ratcheting up bubbling excitement. She'd been planning this surprise for two weeks.

[♬ "Girls Just Want to Have Fun"]

With Jenna's arrival for her summer vacation, Chett's exclusive use of the large property would end. And so would private outdoor shenanigans.

At Jenna's guest cottage, Chett carried the groceries into the kitchen and deposited them on the counter. Meanwhile Catrina snuck a bag containing the costume into his bedroom.

"I'll fix lunch while you take Titan for a short run," she offered.

Chett stretched. "It's warm, but I do need the exercise. We'll stick to the shaded lanes. Sure you don't want to join us?"

"Not this time." She had preparations to make. She kissed him and practically pushed him out the screen door.

Fifteen minutes later, turkey sandwiches made, fruit washed, cans of beer stashed in the freezer to quickly cool, she dashed into the bedroom and stripped. Eagerly she dressed in the new, skimpy two-piece outfit, then swiveled this way and that in front of a full-length mirror. The costume fit perfectly. She flexed biceps gleaming with sunscreen. Weeks of workouts had paid off.

Finally she wrapped the sandwiches in paper napkins, packed the food and chilled beer into a wicker basket, covered it with a dishtowel to thwart the ants, and carried it down the flagstone path to the lake. After placing the basket under a tree in the shade and ditching her flip-flops, she hot-footed in bare feet across the floating dock's sun-warmed planks. At the end she spread a thick beach towel and took advantage of the rare opportunity to sunbathe.

Then she waited.

Seagulls squealed overhead. Waves from the occasional speedboat slapped the edge of the dock and swished up the small sand beach. One peaceful, endless minute followed another. The blazing sun heated her bones. She longed to jump in the lake and cool off. *Patience.*

At last, too hot and too hyped to remain relaxed, she scooted to the edge of the dock, dangled her feet in the cool water, and scanned the lake. Unfortunately a rowboat bobbed a few hundred feet offshore. That did *not* bode well for her plans. She lifted her sunglasses and squinted, discerning two adults with fishing rods. Hopefully they didn't have a pair of binoculars handy.

Then Titan bounded down the flagstone path, leaped across hot sand, and splashed into the water up to his belly for a drink. The dog's appearance signaled Chett's imminent arrival. She knew his routine. He'd take a quick shower after his five-mile jog, then search for her.

Ten minutes later Chett, clad in swim trunks, sandals, and a Muskoka Laker Brew Pub T-shirt, dropped to sit on the dock beside her.

She grinned at him. The familiar physical reaction to his presence kicked in. Warmth pooled down below, her heartbeat tip-tapped, hormones cascaded into her bloodstream, coherent thought drifted away on the light breeze like the scent of his signature musk shaving lotion. How did surgeons and pilots focus on critical tasks when love fogged their brains and swamped their senses? Love was dangerous, she decided.

"New swimsuit?" he asked.

"Not exactly." She scrambled to her feet to pirouette for the 360-degree view.

He whistled his appreciation. "You look like Raquel Welsh in *One Million Years B.C.* Every 70s-era teenage boy's wet dream."

"Me, Tarzana," she corrected, bending at the waist to give him an eyeful of boobs spilling out of the scrap of faux leopard skin tied over one shoulder.

The matching sarong wrapped around her hips barely covered her butt cheeks. He attempted to flip up the bottom edge. "What's under the skirt, Tarzana?"

She skipped out of his reach. "Later, alligator. First I want to show you something. Stay here."

At the opposite end of the small beach, high on a treed bluff, a strong branch of a huge oak tree stretched over the water. On another visit she'd propped a ladder against the trunk, shinnied along the branch, and securely tied a swing rope to the far end.

While Chett watched from the dock, Catrina detached the knotted end of the long rope from a bent nail hook on the tree trunk, tiptoed to grab hold as high as possible, and, with legs lifted out, swung over the lake while hollering the iconic Tarzan yell. Then at the limit of the swing she let go and plunged butt first into eight feet of deliciously cool water. Momentum propelled her downward until one foot grazed the weedy bottom. She pushed off and surfaced, elated.

Over on the dock, Titan's excited barking drowned Chett's convulsed laughter. He wiped his eyes with the bottom edge of his T-shirt.

Gratified, she snagged the end of the rope, swam ashore, and clambered up the slope to the bluff to hook it onto the nail. Her palms stung from rope burn— but yeah, that was fun!

Chett met her on the beach, his grin as wide as Lake Muskoka. "I wish I had my camera." Intelligent blue eyes sparkled with trademark humor that invariably scrubbed away the moody shadows of her occasional nightmares. "You were magnificent." Hooded eyes dipped to the wet fabric clinging to her curves. He reached to pull her in for a congratulatory kiss, and more.

Aware of their audience in the rowboat, Catrina flattened a palm against his chest. With the other hand she pointed to herself, then him. "Me, Tarzana. You, Big Joe."

"Action scene. My favorite." But the words were muffled. He was already striping off his T-shirt. "I've gotta try this."

They took turns flying out over the lake. After half an hour, breathing hard, they collapsed flat on their backs on the warm dock.

"I love you," Chett said to the sky.

Catrina propped herself up on an elbow, tipped her head to one side and waggled a finger in an ear. "What did you say? I've got water in my ears."

He rolled over onto his side, slid familiar seeking fingers along her leg and under the wrap, and angled for her to lip-read. "I love you."

Love. A strong word. One that probably means something different to me than it does to him.

Beyond infatuation and chemistry, true love had longevity. Commitment. Yeah, the sex was fantastic, but in California Chett had a smorgasbord of beautiful women to date. She wasn't buying it.

"Why me?" Every muscle tensed as she awaited his answer.

"The sex is fantastic."

She laughed ruefully. *That's what I thought.*

He witnessed her disappointment, and a switch flipped behind his eyes. He sat up, crossed his legs, and curled a lock of her long wet hair around his finger. "I've told you how gorgeous you are, how much I admire you..." He rubbed a free hand along his jaw. "I've thought about how to explain how I feel. I'm concerned that it'll sound like it's all about me."

Catrina swallowed. "I'm listening."

"Cat, I'm better with you than without you. You reject my BS, challenge me to dig deep and push myself. You won't let me take the easy road. *Sunk* has the most complex characters I've ever written, and that's because I want to please you. Not Jenna. Not Cairncross. *You.*"

She sighed, relaxed. "I get it." And she did. They shored up each other, were stronger together than as individuals. Catrina laced her fingers through his and lifted their linked fists in a victory salute. "Together we tamed our fears."

Chett brought their joined hands to his lips and kissed her fingers. She pressed her mouth to his forehead. "I love you, too."

"I know," he whispered.

She shoved his shoulder, and he laughed, his expression bright with teasing. With love. "I was trying to be romantic," she complained.

"Come back here, Kitten. I'll let you be romantic. Promise." Chett bent to kiss her passionately.

He drove her crazy. Crazy with need. Her girl parts swelled. His male part stiffened.

His hands wandered into a binocular-wary zone. "Hmmm, no underwear."

She reluctantly interrupted the proceedings. "I forgot about our picnic lunch. Are you hungry?"

"Hungry for you," Chett mumbled into the curve of her breast.

Over his shoulder she spied Titan with his snout deep in the wicker basket. She sprang to her feet. "Titan," she roared.

The dog lifted his massive head, the napkin-wrapped sandwich packet in his jaws. But rather than obey, he streaked across the beach, up the path and out of sight.

"Titan ate our lunch." She extended a hand to haul Chett upright. "There's more food in the cottage."

He wrapped an arm around her waist and they walked the length of the dock. "Suits me. There's a bed beside the kitchen."

Off in the distance, Titan barked. She shook her head. "Between you two misbehaving males, I have my hands full."

Chett chuckled. "Just wait 'til we have kids."

"What!"

[♫ "Roar"]

THE END

NOTE TO READERS

There are effective treatments for Post-Traumatic Stress Disorder (PTSD). Chett discovered that Emotional Freedom Techniques (EFT), also known as energy psychology, or "tapping," helped him overcome his fear of dogs. EFT is an emerging therapy that is being used successfully by many psychologists and therapists. EFT has gained credibility since the American Psychological Association accepted it for its members' continuing education.

HOW EFT WORKS

The brain's two small amygdala organs are responsible for memory, emotional reactions, and survival instincts. When the body senses danger, the amygdalae flood the body with fear. Tapping with the fingers on specific acupressure points disrupts the amygdalae's fight, flight or freeze response. Therapeutic success is achieved when a memory, experience, or image no longer triggers emotional reactions such as fear, anger, or anxiety.

Many research papers have validated the speed and effectiveness of EFT for resolving PTSD and phobias. However, successful results are directly attributable to a therapist's experience and skill using this technique. If you do not experience any improvement after three sessions, move on to another qualified professional who has completed EFT/energy psychology training accepted by the American Psychological Association.

LEARN MORE

Leaders in the field of energy psychology include Gary Craig (he created the simplified protocol or "basic recipe"),

Dawson Church, Ph.D.; psychotherapist Carol Look, Ph.D.; clinical psychologist David Feinstein, Ph.D.; and marketing maven Nick Ortner. These experts and others demonstrate tapping in numerous YouTube videos.

ABOUT THE AUTHOR

Growing up, Madelle Morgan, her three sisters, and a menagerie of dogs and cats were lucky to spend every summer at their grandparents' Honey Harbour cottage on Georgian Bay. The beautiful lake-dotted District of Muskoka is known as Canada's Hamptons—a summer playground of the rich and famous. As teens, the sisters straddled upstairs-downstairs worlds, working at resorts by day and partying with the wealthy summer crowd by night…and fell in love.

The *Hollywood in Muskoka* series is for fans of Hollywood and people who vacation at a lake, or wish they did. On www.Pinterest.com/madellem you can view Muskoka images that inspired the stories.

Madelle is retired from an engineering career that inspired *Diamond Hunter*, her debut romantic suspense novel about diamond smuggling in Canada's Arctic. She lives in Ottawa, Canada's capital city.

Sign up for Madelle's occasional newsletter at www.MadelleMorgan.com and receive a copy of a free short story entitled *The Next Big Thing*.

FOLLOW LINKS

Facebook: www.Facebook.com/madellemorganauthor

Twitter: www.Twitter.com/MadelleMorgan

Pinterest: www.pinterest.com/madellem

Wattpad: www.wattpad.com/user/MadelleMorgan

Goodreads: www.goodreads.com/wwwgoodreadscomMadelleMorgan

BookLikes: www.madelle.booklikes.com

LibraryThing: www.librarything.com/author/morganmadelle

BOOKS BY MADELLE MORGAN

Diamond Hunter, Romantic Suspense, 2015

Hollywood in Muskoka Series

Caught on Camera, Book 1, Romantic Comedy, 2016

Seduced by the Screenwriter, Book 2, Contemporary Romance, 2017

Hollywood Hero, Book 3, Contemporary Romance, 2019

Subscribe to MadelleMorgan.com for announcements of new releases, deals and giveaways, and receive a free download of her short story, *The Next Big Thing*.

REVIEWS

Reviews are vital to spreading the word about *Seduced by the Screenwriter*. If you enjoyed this story, please leave an honest review on Goodreads or the site where you purchased it. A sentence or two would be much appreciated!

Coming Soon!

HOLLYWOOD HERO

Hollywood in Muskoka series, Book 3

Contemporary romance, available in 2019

Coming Soon!

Summary

Personal assistant Wendy Davila is in love with her boss, Halden Armstrong, megastar of the *Apollo* superhero film franchise. But she can't compete with the succession of stick-thin blond beauties he's caught and released. Or can she?

Halden asks Wendy to accompany him to buy a wilderness fishing retreat in Muskoka. Alone time! It's her chance to remake her dark-haired, curvy self into his ideal woman and set her hook for Halden.

Halden has been burned by love, and the last thing he wants is a woman like his ex who faked it until she hooked him. Wendy is special, and the trip is an opportunity to explore his feelings for her. However, the Greek god has an Achilles' heel. Can he trust Wendy with a secret that could ruin his career? And will she still care when she learns the truth?

Manufactured by Amazon.ca
Bolton, ON

16434639R00101